Saints and Sinners

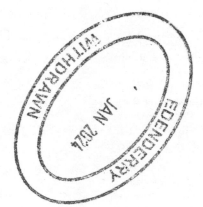

Saints and Sinners

Edna O'Brien

faber and faber

First published in 2011
by Faber and Faber Ltd
Bloomsbury House
74–77 Great Russell Street
London WC1B 3DA

Typeset by Faber and Faber Ltd
Printed in England by CPI Mackays, Chatham

Some of these stories appeared for the first time, in a
slightly different form, in the following magazines: *The New Yorker*,
Zoetrope, *Atlantic Monthly* and *The Sunday Times*

The right of Edna O'Brien to be identified as author
of this work has been asserted in accordance with
Section 77 of the Copyright, Designs and Patents Act 1988

A CIP record for this book
is available from the British Library

ISBN 978-0-571-27031-6

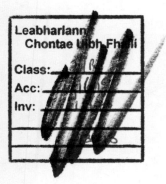
2 4 6 8 10 9 7 5 3 1

For my friend Luke Dodd

Contents

Shovel Kings

In one lapel was a small green and gold harp, and in the other a flying angel. His blue jacket had seen better days. He wore a black felt homburg hat, and his white hair fell in coils – almost to his shoulders. His skin was sallow, but his huge hands were a dark nut brown, and on the right hand he had a lopsided knuckle, obviously caused by some injury. Above it, on the wrist, he wore a wide black strap. He could have been any age, and he seemed like a man on whom a permanent frost had settled. He drank the Guinness slowly, lifting the glass with a measured gravity. We were in a massive pub named Biddy Mulligan's, in North London, on St Patrick's Day, and the sense of expectation was palpable. Great banners with Happy St Patrick draped the walls, and numerous flat television screens carried pictures of the homeland, featuring hills, dales, lakes, tidy towns, and highlights of famed sporting moments down the years. Little votive lamps, not unlike Sacred Heart lamps, were nailed in corners to various wooden beams and seemed talismanic on that momentous day. Only three people were there, the quiet man, a cracked woman with tangled hair gabbling away, and myself.

Adrian, the young barman, was chalking up the promised delights, large Jameson at less than half price, teeny dishes of Irish stew and apple cake for free. Moreover, the governor had left a box full of green woolly hats and green scarves that were reserved to be given to the regular customers. Adrian was young and affable, asking if I needed more coffee and wondering if the quiet man, whom he called Rafferty, would like a refill, in honour of the day. Much to the chagrin of Clodagh, the spry young assistant, Adrian indulged his nostalgia by playing 'Galway Shawl' on the jukebox, over and over again.

The coffee that I had been served was dire, but I lingered, because of being early for an appointment, and picked up a newspaper that was lying on the vacant table next to me. Disaster and scandals featured prominently. Further unrest was reported in a northern province of China; an actress was pictured being helped out of a nightclub in a state of inebriation; another photograph showed her arriving only a few hours earlier wearing a white clinging dress and perilously high heels. A hostage who had been released in some African bush after sixty-seven days in detention seemed dazed by the posse of journalists who surrounded him. I looked at the weather forecast for New York, where I had often spent St Patrick's Day and stood among milling crowds as they cheered floats and bands, feeling curiously alone in the midst of all that celebration.

My appointment was with a doctor whom I had been seeing for the best part of a year and who had just moved to this less salubrious part of London, leaving his rooms in Primrose Hill, probably because of the rents being exorbitant. This would be my first time at this new abode, and I dreaded it, partly because I had left, as I saw it, fragments of myself behind in that other room, with its stacks of books, an open fire, and an informality that was not customary between patient and analyst. Sitting there, with an eye on the wall clock, I kept checking on this new address and asked Adrian about such and such a road to make doubly sure that I had not gone astray. Yes, he knew the man, said he had been in several times, which I took to imply that my doctor liked a drink.

Meanwhile, Clodagh was bustling around in an emerald-green pinafore, reciting a verse for all to hear:

> Boxty on the griddle
> Boxty in the pan
> If you don't eat the boxty
> You'll never get your man.

The light from the leaded-glass panels danced on her shadow as she flitted from table to table, extolling the miracle of the boxty potato bread and dragging a duster over the round brown tables which bore the mottling of years and years of porter stains.

That done, she began to pipe green tincture onto the drawn pints of Guinness to simulate the emblem of the shamrock, something Rafferty observed with a quiet sufferance. A noisy group burst in, decked with leprechauns and green gewgaws of every description, led by a tall woman who was carrying fresh shamrock still attached to a clump of rich earth. In a slightly affected voice she described writing to her old uncle several times since Christmas, reminding him that the plant must not be detached from its soil and, moreover, he must remember to sprinkle it with water and post it in a perforated box filled with loam.

'Was it holy water by any chance?' the cracked woman shouted out.

'Shut your gob,' she was told, at which she raised a hectoring finger, claiming, 'I was innit before yous was all born.'

As the single sprigs of shamrock were passed around, they somehow looked a little forlorn.

A second group followed hot on the heels of the first group, all greeting each other heartily, spreading coats and bags on the various tables and commandeering quiet nooks in the alcoves, for friends whom they claimed were due. A cocky young man with sideburns, wearing a black leather jacket, walked directly to the fruit machine, where the lime-green and cherry-red lights flashed on and off, the lit symbols spinning at a tantalising speed. Two youngsters, possibly his brothers, stood by, gazing and gaping as he fed coin after coin into the machine, and as they waited in vain for the clatter of the payout money, the younger one held an open handkerchief to receive the takings. The elder, who was plump, consigned squares of chocolate into his mouth and sucked with relish, while his brother looked on with the woebegone expression of an urchin.

I had put the newspaper down and was jotting in a notebook one or two things that I might possibly discuss with my doctor when, to my surprise, Rafferty was standing above me and almost bashfully said, 'Do you mind if I take back my paper?' I apologised, offering him a drink, but he was already on his way, detached from the boisterous crowd, carrying himself with a strange otherworldly dignity as he raised his right hand to Adrian in salutation.

Three or four weeks passed before we exchanged a few words.

'What's the harp for?' I asked one morning when, as had become his habit, he made a little joke of offering me the newspaper.

'To prove that I'm an Irishman,' he replied.

'And the angel?'

'Oh that's the guardian angel . . . We all have one,' he said, with a deferential half smile.

About six months after our first meeting I came upon Rafferty unexpectedly, and we greeted each other like old friends. I was on the Kilburn High Road outside a second-hand furniture shop, where he was seated on a leather armchair, smiling at passers-by, like a potentate. He was totally at ease out in the open, big white lazy clouds sailing by in the sky above us, surrounded by chairs, tables, chests of drawers, fire irons, fenders, crockery, and sundry bric-a-brac.

Offering me a seat, he said that the owner believed his presence perked up an interest in business, because once, when he had been singing 'I'll Take You Home Again, Kathleen', passers-by had stopped to listen and, as he put it, had browsed. Nearby, a woman haggled over the price of a buckled sieve, and a young mother was in vain trying to get her son off the rocking horse to which he was affixed. The white paint was scraped in several places, and the golden mane a smudged brown, but to the boy his steed was noble.

Rafferty rolled a cigarette, folded his tobacco pouch, and, impelled by some inner recollection, began to tell me the story of coming to London forty years earlier, a young lad of fifteen arriving in Camden Town with his father and thinking that it was the strangest, sootiest place he had ever seen, that even the birds, the fat pigeons that waddled about, were man-made. Theirs was a small room, which his father had rented the year previous. It had a single iron bed, a thin mattress, a washbasin, and a little gas ring to boil a kettle.

The next morning at the Camden tube station, where lorries and wagons were parked and young men waited to be recruited, literally hundreds of them, hundreds of Irishmen, hoped for a job. A foreman eyed Rafferty up and down and said to his father that no way was that boy seventeen, but his father lied, insisting that he was. More heated words were exchanged, about effing cousins and so forth, but eventually Rafferty was told to climb onto the lorry, and he did. I believed (Rafferty said) that a great future lay ahead of me, but the look of despair on the lads left behind standing in that street was awful, and one I can never forget.

They were driven a few miles north to where a group of young men were digging a long trench, for the electricity cables to be put in later on. The paving stones were already taken up and stacked in piles. At his first sight of it, it was hard for him, as he said, not to imagine those men, young though they were, destined for all eternity to be kept digging some never-ending grave. He was handed a shovel and told to get to work. The handle of the shovel was short, shorter than the ones he had been used to at home when he dug potatoes or turnips, and the blade was square and squat. And so I was (he said) put to digging the blue clay of London, as it was then called, blue from leaking gas and sticky, so sticky you had to dip the shovel in a bucket of water every so often, then wedge it in under the soil to try and shift it. Lads in a line, stripped to the waist because it was so hot, each man given a certain number of yards to dig, four foot six inches wide and four foot six inches deep. The foreman in his green Wellingtons walking up and down, putting the fear of God into us. A brute, and an Irish brute at that. After an hour of digging, I was half asleep over the shovel and only for Haulie, I would have been fired.

He covered for me, held me up. He was from Donegal, said the mountains and the hilly roads made him wiry, and that I'd get used to it. Two Connemara men nearby spoke only the Irish and didn't understand a word others were saying, but they understood the foreman and the ruthlessness of him. I didn't feel hungry, only thirsty, and the cup of milk at half past ten was a godsend. Tea was brewing all day long in a big bucket, but Haulie said it tasted like senna. Teaboy Teddy was in charge of the grub, and men were given potatoes and cabbage for the dinner, except that I couldn't eat. By the time the whistle went in the evening, my hands were bloodied and my back was ready to break. In the room, I fell fast asleep at the little table, and my father flung me onto the bed, boots and all, and went out.

The same drudge every day (he continued), but they talked and yarned to keep the spirits up. They would talk about everything and anything to do with home. One lad caused riots of laughter when, out of the blue, he announced that turnips needed the frost to taste sweet. He got christened Turnip O'Mara instantly. Nicknames meant for greater camaraderie, down there in the trenches, a brotherhood, us against them, the bull of a foreman and the contractors and subcontractors, who were merely brutes to us, downright brutes. We might chance upon treasure. The legend was that someone had found a Roman plate worth hundreds, and someone else dug up a wooden box with three gold crosses, which he pawned. All we found were the roots of trees, embedded and sinewy, the odd coal bill, and rotten shells of gas piping that German prisoners of war had laid in the forties. On Thursdays a Cork man arrived in a green van to hand out the wages, his bodyguard, also a Cork man, wielding a cricket bat in case of robbery. Men felt like kings momentarily. I got four pounds, which I had to hand over to my father, who also made me write a letter to my mother to say how happy I was and how easily I had settled in to life in London. So much so that she wrote and said she hoped I would not acquire an English accent, as that would be faithless.

I really knew nothing of London (Rafferty said, apologetically), nothing except the four walls of the room, the broken springs of the bed, the street that led to where the wagons and lorries picked men up, and the big white, wide chapel with three altars where the Irish priest gave thunderous sermons on a Sunday. I was full of fears, thought everything was a sin. If the Holy Communion touched my teeth I thought that was a mortal sin. After Mass we had a cup of tea in the sacristy and biscuits dusted with sugar. Sundays were awful, walking up and down the streets and looking at the dinginess of the shop fronts and dirty net curtains in upstairs windows, and the old brickwork daubed black. My father went off very early of a Sunday, but I never knew where to.

We had one book on the small shelf in our room. It was by Zane Grey. I must have read it dozens of times. I was so familiar with it that I could picture swathes of purple sage and cottonwood in Utah, outlaws, masked riders, and felons trailing each other in the big open ranges, one area peculiarly named Deception Pass. I think I swore that I would go there, because I missed the outdoors, missed roaming in the fields around home and hunting on Sundays with a white ferret. My poor mother was writing at least twice weekly, pleading with my father to come home, saying that she could not mind children, do farmwork, and take in washing, and, moreover, that she was suffering increasingly from dizziness. Eventually my father announced that he was going home, and shortly before he did, something happened. We were in the room, and the landlady called my father to the telephone, which was in the kitchen. I thought that maybe my mother had died, but no, he came back in whistling and smiling, handed me two and six and told me to go to the Italian restaurant on the high street and stay there until he picked me up. I lingered for three hours, but no sign of him. The place was shutting. They were putting chairs up on the tables, and a woman waited, the mop already sunk in a bucket of water, to wash the floor. When I got back, the bedroom door was locked. I knocked and waited and knocked, and my father shouted at me to go down the hall, into the back garden. Instead I went towards the hall door. Not long after, a tall, blonde woman, wearing a cape, emerged from our room. She was not a patch on my mother. The way she picked her steps, so high and haughty, I could see that she thought herself way above us. She threw me a strange condescending smile. My father went mad when he saw where I was standing. He said nothing, just drew me into the room by my hair, pulled my pants down and beat me savagely. He kept saying the same thing over and over again as he was belting me – 'I'll teach you . . . I'll teach you honour . . . and I'll teach you obedience . . . and I'll teach you to respect your elders. I'll teach you I'll teach you I'll teach you,' raving mad at having been found out.

A good bit after my father went home (Rafferty continued), I started going to the pub. I was feeling more independent then. I'd go to the Greek café that had been renamed Zorba and have rashers and eggs and fried bread. The kitchen was behind the counter, and the Irish lads had taught Zorba to forget the kebabs and stuffed vine leaves and master the frying pan. Then I'd go straight across to The Aran pub, pure heaven, the warmth, the red table lamps, the talking and gassing, getting a pint, sitting down on a stool, without even exchanging a word. Weeknights were quiet, but weekends were rough, always a fight, because everyone got drunk. The fights could be about anything, a girl, a greyhound, grudges, because a foreman had got rid of six men in order to hire men from his own parish, one wrong word, you know and the punches started. First inside the pub, then in the vestibule and finally out onto the street, the two heavyweights vowing murder and the crowd of us on either side of the pavement egging them on, not unlike the time of the gladiators. When things got really bad and they were near beat to a pulp, someone, usually the landlord, would call the cops. If two cops came on foot they did nothing. They stood by, because they wanted to see the Irish slaughter one another. They hated the Paddies. When the Black Maria pulled up, the two men with blood pouring out of them were just thrown into the back, to fight it out before they got to the station. That's what gave us a bad name, the name of hooligans.

You see (he said apologetically), you had to be tough, on the job and off the job, even if you were dying inside. That's how the sensitivity was knocked out of us. But it was still there, lurking. One night in the bar (and here his voice grew solemn) I saw grown men cry. It was like a wake. They were a gang from Hounslow, and they came in shaken and sat silent, like ghosts. Something catastrophic had happened, and they were all part of it, because they saw it with their own eyes. A young man by the name of Oranmore Joe was up on the digger when the hydraulic gave way and the lever slipped. He didn't realise it for some seconds, not until he saw the big steel bucket full of earth hurtling through the air and crashing on top of a fella that was standing underneath. Knocked him to the ground and cut the head off him. Bedlam. Foremen, building inspectors, cops, a blue plastic sheet put around the scene, and men told to go home and report for work the next morning. Not seeing it (Rafferty said), but hearing about it, at first haltingly and then in a burst, brought it to life, the awful spectacle of a severed head and the young man's eyes wide open, as one of them put it, like the eyes of a sheep's head in a pot. The worst of it was that Oranmore Joe and J.J., that was the young man's name, came from the same townland, and Joe had actually got him the job. Was like a brother to him. A collection was taken in the pub to send the remains home. Lads gave what they could. A pound was a lot in those days, but several pound notes were flung into the tweed cap that had been thrown onto the counter. From that night on (Rafferty lamented), Oranmore Joe was a different man. He wouldn't get on a machine again. The company bought a new machine, but he wouldn't get up on it. He took ground work. He'd sit in the pub, pure quiet, just staring. Lads would try to cheer him up and say, 'No problem Joe, no problem, it wasn't your fault.' Except he believed it was. We'd see him thinking and thinking, and then one evening he comes in, in the navy blue suit and the suitcase, whistling, walking around the pub like a man looking for his dog, calling, ducking under the stools and the tables, and then we hear what he's saying. He's saying, 'Come on J.J., we're going home,' and we knew, we knew that he'd lost it, and we wouldn't be seeing him again. A goner. 'Not one, but two lives lost,' Rafferty said gravely.

In the winter of 1962, two years after his father had

gone, he almost had to follow. The snow began to fall on St Stephen's Day and continued unabated for weeks. All outdoor work ceased. Roads and pavements were iced over, the ice so thick that it would break any sledgehammer, and the trenches were heaped with snow. Men were laid off without pay and many headed for the boat. His landlady, a woman from Trinidad, gave him a few weeks' grace, and as luck would have it, he met up with Moleskin Muggavin in the pawnshop, where Rafferty was pawning a pair of silver plated cufflinks, with a purple stone. Moleskin was looking for men to do renovation on a hotel over in Kensington. The work was altogether different. Feeding sand, gravel, cement, and water into a hopper, the knack being to get the mixed concrete out before it settled, while it was still fluid. He and Murph, a two-man band, easier, as Rafferty said, than shovelling the blue clay of London and no foreman. Moleskin was boss, walking around with a pencil behind the ear, slipping out to the pub and the bookmaker's from time to time, since he fancied himself a keen judge of bloodstock. After work Rafferty accompanied Moleskin to a cocktail bar that adjoined a casino. It was there, as he said, that he got the liking for chasers. Moleskin was on first names with all sorts of notorious people and, moreover, had a friendship with a divorcée who lived in a big white stucco house with steps up to it. Every evening around nine or ten they repaired there, with bottles of porter, and the divorcée, in peacock-coloured dresses and ropes of pearl, would be waiting for Moleskin. Pairs of brown felt slippers were inside the door, as their boots were crusted with snow and wet ice. The brown felt stuff (as he said) reminded him of a tea cosy they had at home, the same material, with a white thatched cottage embroidered on it. Large rooms, leading off one another, carpeted heavens. A party was always in full swing, people dancing and sitting on each other's laps, the cocktail cabinet thrown open and, as a particular feature, Moleskin standing by the piano, to give a rendering of 'I'm Burlington Bertie, I Rise At Ten Thirty'. At midnight, a girl dressed as a shepherdess would enter, ringing a glass bell, announcing supper. All sorts of Austrian delicacies, Wiener schnitzel, goulash, apple strudel with spicy jams, and, in deference to Ireland, boiled pigs' feet and cabbage.

The hotel work was expected to last at least nine months, but it unfortunately came to an abrupt end the day Moleskin socked Dudley, the boss's son, and flung him between the joists of a floor onto a bed of rubble. Dudley, in his Crombie coat and tartan scarf, would call unexpectedly to make sure we weren't slacking. He was a namby-pamby, always spouting about Daddy, every other word being Daddy. Daddy was a great man, a compassionate man. Daddy loved Ireland so much that he flew home every Thursday evening, so as to step on Irish soil and be reunited with wife and family. This particular day, when he said that Daddy deserved to have a plaque erected in his honour, alongside the liberator

Daniel O'Connell and famous dead poets, Moleskin erupted and said to cut out the tripe.

After the fracas that ensued, he and Moleskin kept away from the London area for several weeks. Moleskin knew a man who kept a caravan above the beach at Hove, where they holed up, living on bread and sardines. Passing himself off as a landscape gardener, Moleskin got them piecework, and (Rafferty said) he was once more at the mercy of the shovel.

The last he saw of Moleskin was one evening in The Aran after the frozen ground had thawed and he was working for a different set of contractors, jumping on a blue wagon instead of a brown one (he said). Moleskin arrived in a green trench coat and announced that he was leaving London to attend on a lady in Lincolnshire, then proceeded to borrow from all before him and promised to invite them for a shooting weekend.

At times over the years, Rafferty was put to work out of London. Once near Birmingham, where they were building a motorway, and another time outside Sheffield, for the construction of a power plant. The men lived in huge camps, sleeping on straw mattresses and fending for themselves in a communal kitchen. But I always (he said, quite shyly) missed Camden. Camden was where I first came, and though I cried my eyes out in the beginning and walked those hopeless sullen streets, it was where I had put roots down. The odd thing was that you can be attached to a place, or a person, you don't particularly like, and he put it down to mankind's addiction to habit.

It was only when he took his leave of me that I realised that darkness had fallen. The white clouds of a few hours earlier had sallied off, and a star flickered wanly in the heavens. People on foot, in cars, and on bicycles were hurrying with that frenzied speed that seizes them at rush hour, and Rafferty had nothing more to impart. I suggested buying him a drink, but not then, nor at any time in the year that I would come to know him, would he accept hospitality. His last vestige of pride.

After Christmas, in the pub, Rafferty was buoyant. He had had a haircut and was sporting a maroon silk handkerchief in the top pocket of his jacket. He had been 'away', as he put it. Away was only a few miles north, but to him, confined to his own immediate radius, any journey was an adventure. I knew a little of his movements by now. He drank the one pint in Biddy Mulligan's each morning, returning in the evening to have his quota of two. In the day he walked and, as he said, could be a census collector, if only anyone would employ him. At noon he went to the Centre where he, along with several others, were given a cooked dinner and coffee. Roisin, the woman in charge, was a stalwart friend, and every so often gave him a jacket or a pullover, as consignments of clothes were sent from a Samaritan in Dublin, to help the downtrodden Irish in London. Sometimes he helped out a bit in the garden and was even enlisted by Roisin to give sound advice to other young men who might be in danger of slipping.

Christmas he had spent with Donal and Aisling at their pub in Burnt Oak. They were, he said, gallant friends. The pub shut early on Christmas Eve so as to entertain the visitors, which included him, Clare Mick, who lived over Fulham way, and Whisky Tipp, who had had a stroke, but luckily his brain wasn't affected. Also the lodgers upstairs, three Irishmen, a Mongolian, and a black. Pure heaven, as he put it. Up behind the counter and pull your own pint or whatever you wanted. The light in the pub dimmed, the steel shutters drawn, carols on the radio – 'A partridge in a pear tree' – bacon and cabbage for the Christmas Eve dinner, and then, on Christmas Day, as he put it, a banquet. At the start of the dinner, Donal plonked a bottle of champagne in front of each guest, although he and Aisling never themselves touched a drop. What with the roast goose, potato stuffing, sage and onion stuffing, roast spuds, the children larking about, crackers, paper hats, jokes, riddles, and gassing, these dinners were unadulterated happiness. This was how you imagine a home could be, Rafferty said, his voice surely belying the melancholy within it.

One appointment in March with my doctor had been switched to evening. The night was dark and foggy when I got out, and the warm lights of the pub were indeed inviting. The atmosphere was completely different from that of daytime. Such hub and gaiety that, as I entered, I already felt a little intoxicated. Moreover, it was packed. At a large round table a birthday party was in full swing, and a young, obese woman was literally submerged by bunches of flowers and basking in her role as guest of honour. I made my way to the counter where Rafferty was standing and ordered a glass of white wine. Once I had been served, he moved me along to a second counter, where no one was drinking, to avoid the crush. For a while we did not exchange a word. Instead, we studied the array of bottles that were stacked on the top shelf, with their proud labels in gold or black or russet, scored with ornate lettering and coats of arms, testaments to their long lineage. On the lower shelf were the bottles placed upside down, their necks fluting into the clear plastic optics. Every pub, Rafferty said, gave a different measure, and Biddy's was popular because they gave five millimetres extra on a small whisky or vodka. Pondering this for a moment, he said that with drink the possibilities were endless, you could do anything or thought you could. Moreover, time got swallowed up, or more accurately, as he put it, got lost.

A few years after his father went home, his mother died. His father, as he believed, had killed her, had worn her out. The telegram came with the sad news, and he set out, as he said, for Victoria Station, to catch Slattery's coach that fetched passengers to the boat at Holyhead. Never made it. Went on benders along the way in various pubs, lads sympathising with him and saying maudlin things, until the day had turned to night and the coach had left. I'll always regret that I didn't go, he said.

It was quite a while after that the drink got a hold on him, but he knew it was all connected, all part of the same soup. He'd work for six weeks and then booze. Then he'd work the odd day, get a few bob to buy cider, and before long, he was loafing. Mattresses under the bridges, men from every corner of Ireland, gassing at night, talking big in their cups, then arguing and puking in the morning, delirium tremens, seeing rats and snakes, sucking on empty bottles.

One morning (Rafferty continued), I crawled out from under a quilt to go and get a fix. Usually a few people were in the streets going to work or coming from night work, and they'd give you something, especially the women, the women had softer hearts. On the other side of the street I saw a woman in a belted white raincoat looking across at me. It was Madge, who'd married Billy.

She came over, and I can still see her thinking it but not saying it, 'You should see yourself, Rafferty, your dignity gone, your teeth half-gone, your beautiful black hair gone grey, and your eyes glazed.'

I said, 'How's Billy?' and she said, 'Billy's dead and gone,' and her eyes filled up with tears. I could hardly believe it, Accordion Bill that had been such a swank, the two of them such swanks on the dance floor, winning medals and drinking rosé wine. Billy had left the building work after they got the franchise of a pub over in St Martin's Lane, which, as she said, was the ruination of him, of them. Then all of a sudden, she pulled a little notepad from her pocket and thrust it into my hand. This was the chance encounter he believed she had been waiting for, to meet someone from the old days, so that she could show it. Her history, jotted down at different times, often a scrawl and with several coloured inks.

Badly beaten up again. Internal bleeding, rushed to hospital and nearly lost the baby.

Bill not home for three days and three nights, searched up and down the high street, found him in an allotment with other blokes drinking cheap cider, didn't even recognise me, brought him home, cleaned him up, washed him, shaved him, promised to get him new clothes when I got my pay packet.

Billy wept in my arms half the night and I plucked up the courage and I asked him why did he drink like that and his answer was to blank things. I said what things. He said something happened, and that's all he'd say. Something happened. Took it to his grave he did.

Another time I wakened, and he was stuffing pills and whisky down my neck, half unconscious at the time. He wanted to be dead and he wanted us to go together because we loved one another. 'Go together,' I shouted, 'and two young children in the very next room.'

His mother was an Aries. On her seventieth birthday I got him the ticket to go home. I said have a drink, have a few drinks, but promise me you won't get blotto, if you love me,

promise me that, and he did and we hugged. He got to his sis-
ter's house very early in the morning, and the little niece was
pulling at him to put on a CD, and his sister went into the
kitchen to put on the kettle when he collapsed in the door-
way. Never wakened again.

I handed it back, and she said, 'I still love him . . . Will
you tell me why I still love him, Rafferty?' I couldn't.
As she ran to catch the bus she turned back and shouted, 'No one is given a life just to throw it away.' It done
something to me. I went back to the tiny room beyond
Holloway that a priest had got for me. I rarely set foot in
it, because I preferred being under the bridges with the
bums, but I went that morning. There was a mirror I got
off a ship and seeing how I had fallen, I turned its face to
the wall. I started to clean up, emptied things, worn tubes
of toothpaste, eye lotion, old socks, and jumpers and put
them all in a bin bag. Then I got the Hoover from under
the stairs and hoovered, and I poured bleach into a can of
water and scrubbed the windowsills and the woodwork.
Standing in the shower, watching the pictures of little
black umbrellas on the plastic curtain, I made this pact
with myself. I couldn't quit the drink. You could say that
I half won and I half lost. I set myself a goal, one pint in
the morning and two pints at night and not a drop more,
ever, except maybe for a toast at a wedding.

'A woman,' he said, looking at me almost bashfully,
'a woman can do something to a man that cuts deep.
Madge did it, and so did my mother.'

The night before I left home for good (he went on) my mother decided that we would pick fraughans for a pie. They are a berry the colour of the blueberry, but more tart, and they grew in secret places far up in the woods. It was one of those glorious summer evenings, the woods teeming with light, with life, birds, bees, grasshoppers, a sense that the days would never be grey or rainy again. We were lucky. We filled two jugs to the brim, our hands dyed a deep indigo. For some reason my mother daubed her face with her hands and then so did I, and there we were, two purple freaks, like clowns, laughing our heads off. Maybe the laughing, or maybe the recklessness emboldened her, but my mother squeezed my knuckles and said she had something to tell me, she loved me more than anything on this earth, more than her hot-tempered husband and her two darling daughters. It was too much. It was too much to be told at that young age, and I going away forever.

At times, he said after a long silence, he had toyed with the idea of going home, to visit the grave, when he saw Christmas decorations in the shop windows and raffles for Christmas cake, or got the cards from his sisters, who were now grown up and had married young and moved away. Except that he never went. 'If I went home I would have had to kill him,' he said, his sad grey eyes looking into mine, unflinchingly.

*

One Sunday in summer I was enlisted to help at a car-boot sale in a warehouse outside London. Adrian had organised it, so as to collect money to send deprived children to the seaside for a week's holiday. I was assigned to the bookstall – mostly tattered paperbacks with their covers torn off, a few novels, and a book about trees and plants indigenous to the Holy Land, pictures with panoramic views accompanied by beautiful quotations from the Bible. Rafferty was impresario, steering people to the various folding tables, to ransack for bargains. The offerings were motley – winter and summer dresses, worn blankets, quilts, men's shirts, crockery, car tyres, and stacks of old records.

A young nun, her blue nylon veiling fluttering down her back, did brisk business selling cakes, pies, loaves of bread, and homemade jams that had been, as she proudly said, made in the mother house of her order. The other stand that drew a crowd was a litter of young pups in a deep cardboard box, mewling and scampering to get out. They were spaniel and some other breeds. One child, whose birthday it was, lifted his favourite one out, a black and white puppy with a single russet gash on the prow of its head, and as the father handed over two coins, numerous children clamoured for a pet.

Though business was not great, Adrian pronounced it an out-and-out success. We packed the unsold stuff and swept up to give some semblance of cleanliness to the place. As we were being driven back to London in a van, Rafferty asked courteously if I would care for a drink before setting out for home. We got dropped off in a part of London that neither of us was familiar with and that was anything but inviting. Blocks of tall, dun-coloured flats veered towards the sky. They were of such deliberate ugliness their planners must have determined that those who would live in them would do so in unmitigated gloom. A scarlet kite flew above them, sailing in its desultory way, now and then flurrying, as if a sudden swell of wind had overtaken it, and we could not but express the hope that it would never return to the ugly ravine from whence someone, perhaps a child, had dispatched it. Nearby was a playground, more like a yard, bordered with a line of young poplars, beyond which youths yelled and shouted at one another as they played different ball games, the taller ones converged around a basketball net. Dogs ran around, barking ceaselessly.

We could see the sign for a pub, but the entrance eluded us. It was tucked in between a Catholic church, which we recognised by the cross on its grey-blue spire, and a community centre for youths, but though we went up and down several flights of concrete steps and under dark, foul-smelling concrete archways, we kept returning to the same spot. A young Irishman in shorts offered to be of assistance, but said we must first have a peep in the window of the Catholic church, because the altar, brought from Europe centuries previous, was priceless. The church was locked, as evening mass had been said.

We looked through a long stained-glass window and saw an empty room with only a few pews. The altar, set back from the wall, had intricate sprays of gold leaf and was flanked with stout gold pillars. He was a most talkative young man, and pointing to the vista of flats, he listed the crimes that were rife there. He was a community worker and helped the local priest, whom he pronounced his hero. With ebullience, he produced a map of the area, where, with green drawing pins, he had highlighted the scene of three murders, all connected with drugs. Then he descanted, as might an aficionado, on the type of drugs that were being sold, their quality, and the astronomical prices they fetched. He asked us to guess how many languages were current in the neighbourhood and then answered for us, more than twenty languages, and the Irish no longer in the majority, many having gone home and many others having become millionaires.

We thanked him for conveying us, but he was already off on another tangent about some delinquent who passed himself off as blind and was actually a brilliant pickpocket. Inside the pub we had the greatest difficulty getting rid of him and only after Rafferty whispered that we had an important matter to discuss did he take his leave of us, but not before he gave us his business card, printed with his name, a degree in ecology, and his availability as a tour guide of the area.

The place was completely empty. The faint straggling rays of the setting sun came through the long, low win-

dow, and fiddle music filtered from the kitchen area.
Tapping one foot, Rafferty listened, listening so intently
he seemed to be hearing it there and then, and also hearing it from a great distance, rousing tunes that ushered
him back to the neon purlieu of the Galtymore Dance
Hall in Cricklewood, where they had modern and fiddle.
Saturday nights. Admission two shillings and sixpence.
Scores of young men, including him, togged out in the
navy suit, white shirt, and savvy tie, standing at the edge
of the dance floor, gauging the form. One girl was called
Grania, after a pirate queen. Other girls wore bright
flashy frocks or skirts with stiffened petticoats, but Grania had on a black dress with a white collar and inlaid
white bib, giving the appearance of being a nurse. As he
learned later, she was a seamstress in a shop on Oxford
Street, making curtains and doing alterations. What first
struck him, apart from her pure white skin and thick
brown hair, with hues of red and gold like an autumn
bogland, was how down-to-earth she was. Between
dances she would sit, fling off her shoes, and mash her
feet to ready herself for the next bout on the floor. Up at
the mineral bar, other men would be buying her lemon-
ade and pressing her for the next dance, and the one after
that, and she was always saucy with them. He himself
never got on the floor, because of an unconquerable shyness. Six months or more passed before she threw him a
word, and as long again before she allowed him to walk
her home. She lodged three miles beyond Cricklewood,

near Holloway Fields. He recalled standing outside her digs till one or two in the morning, hearing her soft voice as she bewitched him with stories. Listening to her was like being transported. Her father was a tailor who also had a pub and grocery, where people drank, mulled over the latest bit of gossip. She herself preferred when one of the old people, from up the country, happened to come in and told stories of the long ago, cures and curses, warts removed by being rubbed with black stones taken out of the bed of the river, and the wonders of Biddy Early the witch who, by gazing into her blue bottle, reached second sight.

He would drink in the week evenings, but kept himself fairly sober on the Saturdays, to gaze at Grania, to buy her the minerals and walk her home. One night when they were parting she handed him a gift in a sheet of folded paper and whispered a few words in Irish. This was her way of saying she was his.

Next morning he studied the gift again and again. It was a smooth flattened seashell, the ribs on the underside, bone white, curving out into a fan, and in the interstices, tiny vermilion shadings like brush strokes, as if someone had painted them on.

They found a little flat above a hardware shop that was many miles from Camden. Friends donated things, sheets, bolsters, and a jam dish with a hanging spoon that carried a coloured likeness of His Holiness the Pope. Soon he learned what a fine cook Grania was, but she was also very particular. For their Sunday walk, she would not let him out with a crease in his shirt, having already cleaned the clay under his nails with a crochet needle. The thing was (as he ruefully put it) Grania could drink any man under the table, but she knew when to stop. In the evenings when he got home, two glasses of milk would be on the table, to have with the dinner. But he was missing the pub, the noise, the gas, and before long he would be dropped off at The Aran and have a few drinks and arrive home late. Then later. Soon he pretended he was on overtime, and would not be home till midnight. A row would often follow, or else Grania would have gone to bed, his dinner, with a plate over it, on a rack above the gas cooker. One night he got back and found a note on the kitchen table – 'You can have your overtime, now and forever,' was all it said. He thought she would be back the next evening, or the next, but she wasn't.

'She took nothing, not even the jam dish with the hanging spoon and the likeness of the Pope,' he said, then broke off abruptly. One of the dogs from the playground had come in and was staring up at us, panting wildly. Rafferty put his hand on its snout and kept it there until the animal's breathing had quieted, and in the silence, I was conscious for the first time of a ticking wall clock.

Considering the plethora of crimes we'd been warned of, I suggested taking a minicab and offered to drop Rafferty home.

'Most kind,' he said, which I knew to be his way of

declining, followed by his raising the large hand, with the black, wide wristband.

We were out of doors, sitting, as it happened, on a bench, in a graveyard that was anything but morose. A wide bordered path ran from a gateway to another at the opposite entrance, allowing a shortcut for pedestrians and cyclists, so that it was as much a haunt of the living as of the dead. The graves were neatly tended, the grass bank on the far side newly mowed, and there was the added gaiety of springtime in London. Borders of simmering yellow tulips, front gardens and back gardens surpassing each other in bounteous displays, the wisteria a feast in itself, masses of it falling in fat folds, the blue so intense, it lent a blueness to the eyes themselves. Adrian had said that Rafferty would love a few moments with me if it was possible and hinted that he had super-duper news.

He could not contain his joy. He was going home. For good. No more bills. No more hassle. Then he took the letter from his leather wallet that was worn and crinkled, but hesitated before handing it to me, since he needed to explain the circumstances. A benefactor, who had begun life digging, but who had bettered himself and accrued great riches, had contacted the Centre, asking for someone of good character to come home to Ireland and take care of an elderly relative. Roisin, being the stalwart she was, had suggested Rafferty, and after a ream of letters, his credentials, etcetera, passed on, he was accepted. Moreover, she had given him a new tweed suit and pullover, since a fresh consignment had come from the Samaritan.

The house, the dream house or bungalow to where he was going, would be shared with the elderly man, but a woman was coming in every day to do the dinner and keep an eye on the elderly man's needs, since he suffered from diabetes, something which he contracted later in life. Rafferty must have read the benefactor's letter dozens of times, as it had been folded again and again. Forty years previously, when he left Ireland, his mother, his lovely mother, had packed his things in a brown suitcase, and he had taken his belongings out, except for three sacred things: a missal, a crucifix, which she had had blessed, and striped pyjamas, which he never wore, but had kept in case he had to go to hospital. He was lucky to have escaped that, because many of his mates were struck down with chronic illnesses, asthma, lung diseases, skin diseases, and injuries of every kind. He said he would humour the elderly relative, whom he guessed would sleep half of the day, or at least doze. He would play cards with him, or maybe do crosswords. With a vigour, he contemplated picking up a shovel again and getting a bit of garden going – cabbage, sprouts, shallots, lettuce – and see what potatoes were native to that particular soil. 'I'll go to the pub,' he said, 'stands to reason, but I'll pace myself, no going back to skid row for Rafferty.' The bungalow was not in his own part of the country, but still it was home and he asked out loud if it was likely that he would once again hear the cry of the corncrake, that distinctive call which had never faded from his memory.

Birds in their truant giddiness were swooping and scudding about the gravestones, but a few pugnacious ones had converged on a plastic lunch box that had the remains of a salad, and were conducting bitter warfare by brandishing torn shreds of limp lettuce. Their beaks were a bright, hard orange.

When I am sitting on a rocking chair over there, on the borders of Leitrim and Roscommon (he continued), and they ask me how it was in the building work, I'll tell them it was great, great altogether, and I'll tell them about Paddy Pancake. Shrove Tuesday we were all on site, itching to get off early, because we'd sworn to give up drink for Lent. Paddy Pancake sprung a surprise on us. Never touched a drink himself, and wore his total abstinence badge for all to see. He was a night chef, somewhere in Ealing. From a black oilskin bag he took out flour, eggs, milk, caster sugar, salt, and a small bottle of dangerous-looking blue liqueur. He'd even brought a basin to make the batter. Then, looking around, he picked up a big shovel, washed it down a couple of times with a hose, and presto, he had his frying pan. Two lads were told to get a fire going, as plenty of wood from timbers and old doors was scattered on a nearby site. Paddy tossed the pancakes on the shovel like a master. He had an assistant to sprinkle on the caster sugar and a few drops of the liqueur, and lads grabbed and gobbled like wolves. To crown it all, a shy Galway boy stood up on a skip and belted out a rebel song, 'Roddy McCorley Goes to Die on the Bridge of Toome Today'. The words and his voice so beautiful, so heartfelt.

Tears welled in his eyes as he recalled that revel, a winter evening, the glow of the fire, the leaping flames of red and blue, dancing in that London wasteland, as if in some roman amphitheatre.

As he tucked the letters back in his wallet, a photo of himself fell out. It was a snap really, taken on some riverbank, where he and his friends had obviously been swimming. The sheer life in his expression was breathtaking. His hair was tousled. His eyes as youthful and moist as any young man's eyes could be. Not a single feature in that photograph resembled the man sitting beside me.

'Well, that's youth for you,' he said, suddenly bashful, as I had guessed, it was a fleeting farewell.

Less than two weeks later, when I called into the pub, for a moment I thought that I must be hallucinating. Sitting in his usual place, with a pint on the table in front of him, was a man the spitting image of Rafferty. Same wide-brimmed black hat, wrinkled jacket, and the pint. I looked away, but then Adrian gave me the nod, and I looked again. It was Rafferty. It was him. He was quiet

and took his time before he acknowledged me, showing none of the warmth that he had on that day in the
graveyard. 'It happens,' he said, then taking his leave, the
unfinished pint on the table, he added that the rolling
stone gathers no moss.

Adrian relayed to me what had happened. The bungalow was new and clean, too new and too clean. The
old man, Denny, sat in his chair all day looking out at
the low-lying fields, invariably shrouded in mist, checking his blood sugar every few hours, having an insulin
injection, and taking four different sets of tablets. A Miss
Moroney came to do the dinner, and drove them mad.
The landing was like a shrine, with statues, Miss Moroney spouting homilies about the evils of drink and touching them for alms for unfortunate children in the third
world. Even when he went to the pub, Rafferty didn't
feel at home. It was noisy and brash, young people coming and going, no quiet corner to brood in, and no one
had any interest in his stories. As for the garden that he
had intended to plant, the grounds around the house
had been landscaped with bushes and yellow flowering
shrubs. Nothing was wrong, as he told Adrian, but nothing was right, either. The benefactor took the news of his
sudden departure well, said he could come for a week in
the summer if he wished, and that he had no hard feelings. The same young minicab driver who had collected him from the airport was the one to bring him back
again, drove like a lunatic while also conducting a busi-

ness transaction on a mobile phone, telling the would-be purchaser to get stuffed, that no way would he take two hundred. Seconds later he rang someone else to report on matters, saying that they would be mad to let it go for less and they would hold out for the jackpot. According to Adrian, Rafferty surmised that it was either a motor-cycle or an old banger that was for sale. At the airport, the minicab driver mashed his hand in effusive farewell and said what a pity the holiday had been so short.

Roisin had persuaded the council to give him his lit-tle room back, and, as Adrian said, the brown suitcase with the missal, the crucifix, and the striped pyjamas was shoved back under the single bed.

'He doesn't belong in England and ditto Ireland,' Adrian said, and, tapping his temple to emphasise his meaning, added that exile is in the mind and there's no cure for that.

I was flabbergasted the day my analyst broke the news to me that he was leaving London and going to work in a hospital in Bristol. With solicitude he had procured a railway timetable and showed me how frequently the trains ran, saying I could come twice a month and have a double session.

I went back to the pub, to say goodbyes of a sort. Adri-an treated me to an Irish coffee, and Rafferty came across and stood by us, as Adrian recounted his big night at the greyhound track in Wimbledon, picking four winners because of tips that he got from the barmaid, a Connemara girl, whom he hoped to be seeing again.

'Mind yourself.' Those were the last words Rafferty said to me. He did not shake hands, and, as on the first morning, he raised his calloused right hand in a valediction that bespoke courtesy and finality. He had cut me out, the way he had cut his mother out, and those few who were dear to him, not from a hardness of heart, but from a heart that was immeasurably broken.

Under the pavement were the lines of cable that linked the lights of the great streets and the lesser streets of London, as far distant as Kent. I thought of the Shovel Kings, and their names suddenly materialised before me, as in a litany – Haulie, Murph, Moleskin Muggavin, Turnip O'Mara, Whisky Tipp, Oranmore Joe, Teaboy Teddy, Paddy Pancake, Accordion Bill, Rafferty, and countless others, gone to dust.

Sinners

They were in. Mother, father, and daughter. Delia had stayed awake to hear them come in, but she would be awake anyhow, since sleep eluded her more and more as the years went on. Occasionally, she would fall asleep unbeknownst to herself and waken in that grim hour before dawn and, going to the window, she would see her dog come from under the hedge, tuned to the first, almost imperceptible sound inside the house, and look up at her with knowing eyes, asking that she come down, open the back door, and serve it its usual saucer of tea with milk.

Sometimes she took a tablet, but dreaded being at the mercy of any drug and had a secondary dread of one day not being able to afford them. In her wide-awake vigils, she prayed or tried to pray, but prayer, like sleep, was on the wane now, at the very time when she should be drawing closer to her blessed Maker. The prayers came only from her lips and not from deep within anymore. She had lost that most heartfelt rapport that she once had with God.

So at night, awake, she would go around the house in her mind and think of improvements that she would make to it in time – new wallpaper in the good room, where the existing pink was stained around the window frames, brown smears from repeated damp. Then in the vacant room where apples were stored, the wallpaper had been hung upside down and had survived the years without any visitors noticing that the acorns and hummingbirds were the wrong way around. She might have it replaced also, just to get the better of those bostoons who had hung it incorrectly. Delia was a woman who liked to be always in the right. Funny, that on the day the paper was being hung she had consulted a fortune-teller in the city about a certain matter and had been told that she would go home and find that those birds and acorns were upside down and to her dismay, she did. In other quarters of the house she was more spartan with her envisaged improvements – she thought maybe a new strip of linoleum inside the hall door, to save the tiles from trampling boots and wellingtons. Scrubbing was hard for her now, especially hard on her lower back. Then there were little requirements, such as new towels, tea towels, and dishcloths. The dishcloths smelt of milk, no matter how thoroughly she soaked or boiled them. They had that sour, gone-off smell.

Smell was Delia's strongest sense and when these paying guests arrived that morning, she smelt the woman's perfume and the daughter's, identical, and yet nothing else about them seemed similar. The daughter, Samantha, was cocksure, with toffee-coloured hair, narrowing her eyes as if she were thinking something mathematical, when all she was thinking was, 'Look at me, spoil me.' Her long hair was her chief weapon, which she swept along the table as she scrutinised the wallpaper, or a picture over the whatnot of pussycats who were trying to move the hands of a clock close to feeding time. She kept insisting that her parents have a bite of the iced cake, because it was yummy. Although the price quoted only included bed and breakfast, Delia liked to give her guests a cup of tea when they arrived and whatever cake happened to be in the tin. Samantha's short skirt drew attention to her thighs, which were like pillars of solid nougat inside her cream lace stockings. She wore two-tone shoes that buttoned across the instep. The mother was dark and plump, and made a habit of touching the daughter whenever she jumped up in one of her fits of exuberance. The father smoked a pipe. He was a handsome man, tall and distant, and who seemed like a professor of something.

After the tea and cake, they wondered if they might have a picnic basket with some sandwiches and hardboiled eggs as they were taking a boating expedition. She explained then that they must make their own arrangements for dinner, as she was really just bed and breakfast.

When they returned, after midnight, she heard them say 'Shhh shhh shhh' repeatedly as they climbed the stairs. They used the bathroom in turn. She could tell by their footsteps and had to concede that they were doing their best to be quiet, that is, until something went crash,

crash. She reckoned it was the china tooth mug. She loved that tooth mug, cream with green fluting and little garlands of shamrock, and she wanted to get up and tackle them, but something stopped her. Also, she did not have a dressing gown. Would they be in their dressing gowns? The woman possibly yes, and the man in his shirtsleeves. She would miss that tooth mug, she would mourn it. Her things had become her faithfuls, what with all else gone or scattered. She knew, yes, she knew, that the love from children became fainter and more intermittent with time, not unlike a garment washed and rewashed, until it is only a suggestion of its original colour. Their daughter, their Samantha, would be like that soon, would skedaddle once she had other interests, boyfriends and so forth.

The parents had the blue room, which had been her and her husband's bridal room, the one where her children were born and where, as the years went on, she slept as little as possible, visiting her husband only when she was compelled to and afterwards washing and rinsing herself thoroughly. Five children were enough for any woman. Four scattered, one dead, and a daughter-in-law who had made her son, her only son, the essence of graspingness. Still, she must not be too hard on them, too judgemental. The girls remembered when they remembered, they sent gifts, especially the youngest daughter, and next time, when asked what she wanted for her birthday, she would say a dressing gown so that she could confront her lodgers in a crucial moment.

She only kept people in summer, partly because that was when tourists came, but also to heat the whole house in winter would be extravagant, as oil was so expensive. Moreover, she never kept people for more than two or three nights, believing they might get forward and start to think that the house was theirs, opening wardrobes and drawers, finding the souvenirs of her past, hand-kerchiefs with mottos embroidered on them, a lavender dance frock and coatee, and a fan of black gauze with an ebony handle. Her other reason was more covert. She was afraid she might grow attached to them and ask them to stay longer, for the company. With the tak-ings from summer guests she made improvements to the house and the grounds, and her only luxury was a large tin of raspberry and custard biscuits, for which she had a kind of craving.

Yes, the couple were in her marriage bed, a wide bed with an oak headboard that rattled, and a rose-coloured quilt that she had made during her betrothal, stitching all her dreams into it. She imagined them, professorial man and plump wife, lying side by side, the square pouches of the quilt rising and sinking with their breathing, and she remembered the clutching of it as her husband made wrathful and unloving love to her. With the years he had become a little kinder, the husband she would have wished for at the outset, and he never touched a drink after the age of fifty-five, which was why she indulged him by making him tea at all hours of day and night.

Samantha was probably not asleep, but shaping her eyebrows or brushing the long spill of hair, brushing it slowly and maybe surveying herself in the wardrobe mirror, admiring her plump, firm little figure inside her short nightgown. After they went out to dinner, she had peered into their rooms. She did not open their suitcases, as a point of honour, but she studied some of their possessions – the woman's string of pearls, her cosmetics, and a dark brown hairnet lying stealthily next to her husband's pipes, pipes of different coloured wood and a folded swag of mulchy tobacco. Their money, their English money, was piled into two little neat banks, his money and her money, as Delia felt. On the girl's dressing table there was only a hairbrush, cotton buds, and a bottle of baby oil. The diaphanous pink nightie was laid out on her pillow and looked life-like, or as if there were a doll inside it.

Sleep would not come.

She got up, intending to go and look at the broken tooth mug, but as soon as she reached the door something prevented her. She was ashamed of being heard by them and it was as if the house had become theirs. She had some peculiar reservation about them, how over-friendly they were with each other and blowing about what a brilliant hol they were having, yes, something unnerved her. She paced in her room. She could not go into the hall and pace, as was her habit, and put her hand on the cold plaster statue of the Virgin, asking for protection.

Exactly half an hour after they had retired, it happened. She heard a creak, then the girl's door opening slowly and she thought it was a bathroom need, but instead she heard her go towards the parents' room on tiptoe, then a tap, a series of taps, light and playful, not the tapping of a sick or over-wrought child, not the tapping of a child frightened by dark, or disturbed by a crow in the chimney, not that at all, and in seconds, Delia twigged. Her whole body stiffened in revulsion. She heard the girl go into their room and then she was out of bed, her hand on her own doorknob, opening it very softly, as she moved across the landing barefoot, in their direction, not knowing exactly what she would do. The whole house listened. They were not talking, yet something appalling was transpiring in there, whispers and tittering and giggles. She could not see, yet her eyes seemed to penetrate through the panelled door as if it were transparent, and she pictured them, their hands, their mouths, their limbs, all seeking one another out. They had not dared to put on a light. The girl was probably naked and yielding, allowing them to fondle her, the man fondling her in one way, the woman in another, and before long she knew that it would reach the vileness of an orgy. She would have to go in there and catch them out – the man, lord of his harem, straddled over a girl who was in no way his daughter, and the woman ministering, because that was the surest way she could hold onto a husband. This was no daughter of theirs. Maybe

43

she was a hitchhiker to whom they had given a lift, or perhaps they had placed an advertisement, the words cunningly couched, in their local paper, in the Midlands of England, where they came from, or where they said they came from. There was a poker in that room, laid into the coal scuttle, left there since her last confinement thirty years previous, and she was already picking it up and breaking it on their bare, romping bodies. What detained her she could not say. Everything determined that she could go in and yet she faltered. Then came the exclamations, the three pitches of sound so different — the woman's loud and gloating, the girl's, helpless, as if she were almost crying, and the man, like a jackass down in the woods with his lady loves. She hurried back to her room and sat on the edge of her bed, trembling. From a little round box in her bedside drawer, she felt for the sleeping tablet that was turquoise in colour, identical to the sea on a postcard that her youngest daughter had once sent from the Riviera. For thrift's sake she halved it, she always halved them. The powder on her tongue tasted bitter, poisonous, and she had no glass of water to wash it down.

Sleep came and with it a glut of dreams. She was with a group of women who were about to be photographed by two men, obvious rivals who bickered and elbowed each other out of the way. For the actual photograph all were ordered to undress, but she could not, she would not. Stoutly she refused to remove her camisole, which was of coarse, unbleached linen. The woman next to her, whom she recognised as Ellie, the local dressmaker, did undress and waddled about as would a hussy. Then suddenly the dream shifted. She was alone in a big church that was regal, but very profane. The saints, Joseph and Jude and Anthony and Theresa the little flower, were all stripped of their robes and if that was not sacrilege enough, the priest sang lustily, as if he were in a beer garden. Then a little altar boy in cardinal red started to prance about and help himself to wine from the chalice. She kept believing that she was not dreaming, except that she was. When she wakened suddenly, at once she remembered the paying guests, their panting, the vile happenings and how she would have to fry rashers and eggs and sausages for their loathsome breakfasts.

She threw her clothes on, fumbled with her stockings, which would not draw up as quickly as they should, and swept her hair back severely with side combs.

Their breakfasts were on the table for when they sat down – the fry, a pot of tea, a jug of hot water, and a jug of instant coffee. She had also left a small dish of mandarin oranges. They were to help themselves. Often with guests, she would linger in the breakfast room and learn of faraway places – the coral reefs, or the wildly contrasting climates in different parts of Australia, or Table Mountain in Cape Town, where it seemed the condensation formed a tablecloth of cloud over the flat plateau. But she did not talk to this bunch, did not even pop her head through the door to ask if they required more toast or more coffee.

It was as they were leaving that she took her revenge. There they were, a family tableau of harmlessness, with their suitcases, the wife's of black fibre, the girl with a blue rucksack, and the husband with a brown leather attaché case. She was, as she said, only charging them for the one room, since, by her reckoning, only one room was fully occupied. She saw that they understood, but chose maddeningly not to react. The husband handed her a five-pound note, some single notes and silver that covered the cost of the two rooms. She insisted he take some back, but he refused, as did his wife. It got quite spiteful then. The husband showed his displeasure by baring his teeth and the wife remarked on the scarcity of towels in the bathroom and as for the jerky, antediluvian lavatory chain, that went out with the Ark. The daughter smirked as she sucked on tiny crescents of mandarin orange. Eventually, the husband thrust the three notes and the coins inside the dipping pocket of her overall and determined not to be outdone, she hurled them lasso-wise along the chipstone gravel. The coins glittered in the bright morning sunshine.

They were on the other side of the gate now, the parents putting the luggage into the boot, when the daughter ran back to pick up the money, then stuck her tongue out in brazen defiance.

She watched until the car was well out of sight. Then

she flopped onto the grass and began to cry. She cried from the pit of her being. Why was she crying? Why am I crying, she asked aloud. It was not over them or the unsavouriness of the night. It was to do with herself. Her heart had walled up a long time ago, she had forgotten the little things, the little pleasures, the give and take that is life. She had even forgotten her own sins.

The grass was soft and silken and not too dry, nourished from rain and spells of sunshine.

Madame Cassandra

At last at last. I have been perambulating for the best part of an hour . . . luckily I had my brolly to keep off that glaring sunshine. It must be at least twenty-three Celsius . . . the poor earth is baked . . . even the old weeds are passing out and the foxglove expiring. I always love the way the bees snuggle into the foxglove . . . for the coolth and the nectar . . . make themselves at home – 'Where the harebell grows and the foxglove purple and white' . . . a favourite . . . from the anthologies.

My, my . . . what a pretty caravan . . . so gaily coloured and flowers, flowers. Steps painted in three different shades. 'Madame Cassandra' – how beautiful, how ancient. You know your mythology I am glad to see. It says 'No appointment necessary' but Madame your door is shut . . . your half door is shut and your heavy red curtain is drawn all along your picture window. I am a little weary . . . trudging here and so forth . . . not to mention the inconvenience of having to ask people directions, when I alighted from the bus. I shall rest a little on one of your steps, on one of your painted steps.

Eureka. I know what it is . . . you are expelling, if that is the word, the karma of the previous incumbent and a good thing too . . . I must say I would love a glass of water

or a glass of angostura bitters . . . such a thirst – parched.
I see you collect stones, large stones, small stones, rocks,
and that fearsome boulder . . . I expect each has a signifi-
cance for you, a hidden power. Those ponies are pretty
and dappled, but wild . . . wild and quite unpredictable.
It must be common ground . . . I noticed people – strays,
youths, louts – and one or two caravans, much drabber
than yours. To tell you the truth I am quite breathless . . .
I have been over yonder for the last hour . . . I saw that
you were occupied . . . I saw your sign – 'Do Not Dis-
turb'. Made myself scarce. The previous client . . . I happen to know her. We are, neighbours. Her people's land
abuts onto our avenue which of course is more exclusive
what with our belt of trees, yews, and cypresses that have
matured down the years. Good lady, I imagine that you
are resting . . . it stands to reason . . . you are drained.
When a young girl, may I say a buxom young convent
girl such as your last client, comes for advice it is usually pertaining to matters of the heart . . . Comprendé. I
hope you don't mind my sitting here and gabbling away
. . . it lessens the fret. I shall try to admire the surroundings . . . though to be honest I would rather I were not
observed. Matters of the heart must be strictly confidential. Comprendé. I am Mildred . . . wife of Gerhardt,
Mr Gentleman . . . my maiden name was Butler . . . we
are descended from the House of the Ormonds . . . our
flower gardens and our fruit gardens were renowned –
open on certain summer Sundays to the public whence

teas were served in a little summerhouse. As a matter of fact Mr Gentleman wooed me in the kitchen garden, in and out between the raspberry canes and the loganberry canes and the tall delphiniums. Many girls, it seems, had set their caps on him, this young and eligible barrister, set their caps on him to no avail. My yearning was for the stage . . . how I loved the magic, the make-believe. Even at the age of six or seven when my mother took me to the Gaiety Theatre in Dublin for the pantomime and we sat in a box, I drank it all in – the orchestra, the miming, the intrigues, the dames, the villains, the skits and the ever-happy ending. My father would wait for us at his club in Stephen's Green, and we would have dinner in a very salubrious dining room. I played Desdemona in my boarding school . . . Othello, well she/he was somewhat uncouth . . . ah yes, one who loved not wisely but too well. So when I met Gerhardt I was full of Desdemona but not for long. You see my heart went on a ninety-mile . . . what is it called . . . revolve. I lost my head. I waited for the ring of our garden bell. Oh what a chirpy sound from that big fat copper bell . . . Mr G coming on any excuse, the flimsiest of excuses, in a suit or in old dungarees and always when least expected . . . how the heart registers these thunderbolts. I was much younger and younger still for my actual years . . . yes, in and out between the raspberry canes, and the loganberry canes and would you believe it our dog Hector got so jealous he would bark and chase Mr Gentleman, in

venom, and one day he took a great scoop out of the side
of Mr Gentleman's hand, kept his teeth there, and what
did Gerhardt do . . . he did a strange thing, a rather cru-
el thing – he kicked Hector, beat him into submission,
and Hector became his friend . . . Mr Gentleman could
handle beast or man or woman or girl . . . In time he
was welcomed indoors . . . a sherry and so forth . . . his
pursuit of me was both adamant and subtle, which was
why they thought him ideal. He always brought gifts –
chocolate or cherry brandy truffles – he was one-eighth
foreign, Normandy stock, which added to his mystique.
He proposed in a country churchyard and it was dusk
and there was not a soul about . . . just like the elegy –
'the lowing Herd winds slowly o'er the Lea' – and he
made a ring of grasses . . . a magic ring, engagement and
eternity so to speak. A couple of nights before our wedding he was in the library with my father . . . they had
become bosom friends or should I say bosom buddies –
they played backgammon, they reminisced, they drank
port or Armagnac – in those days I did not drink . . . slept
like a baby . . . whereas now the evening tipple is man-
datory. I overheard them speak of women – how much
they loved women, idealised women – dilated on their
necks, their sloping shoulders, their hindquarters, their
ankles . . . all very detached . . . almost clinical . . . my
father did not mention my mother, Alannah, not once.
Stressing how certain pieces of music reminded them of
their trysts with certain women, either because the music

was being played on a gramophone in some lady's drawing room or perhaps, some more . . . obtuse reason, my
dear mother . . . so beholden. I could always tell when
they had been intimate because next morning my father
would be most imperious, quite snappy, munching his
toast . . . crumpling his newspaper, and my mother a tri-
fle foolish and obliging. Yes I stood in the doorway half
expecting my husband-to-be or my father to say 'Ah Millie come in' but they didn't, either because they were so
engrossed and did not see me or else they thought my
presence was inappropriate. Madame I know you are
resting . . . each séance, each session, call it what you will,
must take a lot out of you, reaching into the soul of the
person and drawing out the inmost secret, the kernel.

Perhaps you are praying – 'And death shall be no
more, nor mourning, nor crying, nor sorrow shall be any
more.' I regard myself lucky to have found you, to have
tracked you down . . . now where was I . . . oh yes, oh
yes our wedding . . . it was beautiful . . . it was written
up in more than one daily newspaper . . . the smell from
the lily of the valley drenched the little country church
in County Waterford . . . our own lily of the valley at
that – tiaras of it for the bridesmaids and bunches for the
little maidens of honour – it was intoxicating . . . a choir
. . . hymns . . . me poured into my ivory slipper-satin. My
husband could not take his eyes off me that June morning
. . . I should like for a moment to say something about my
husband's eyes . . . they are in the normal course of things,

as he broods over his papers and his briefs, they are not
unlike an oyster, which is to say that they are grey with
a milkyness . . . but when, as for instance our wedding
morning, when the dart of Cupid has struck, they are
opal, which is to say they have the merest hue of silver,
limned with blue . . . I saw them then and many other
times and . . . and I see them now and they are not on me
and they are not for me and it is awful . . . and it is awful.
Our honeymoon was . . . well it was sailing into the sunset
. . . pure bliss . . . unadulterated bliss . . . there is no other
word quite so appropriate . . . or so nuanced, devoid of
affection and small talk. But which does one want more,
bliss or affection, and moreover I had brought a stack of
books . . . the Aegean Sea a palette of blues . . . and all
those guidebooks with tales of the ancients, the gods and
the goddesses . . . what spitfires they were . . . with their
intriguings . . . always plotting to get the upper hand of
one another . . . if Hera liked you, Athena didn't, and
Juno marrying her own brother Jupiter, who wooed her
in the guise of a cuckoo . . . not to mention old Poseidon
. . . who could stir up a storm in a flash . . . yes . . . essential
to keep on the good side of Zeus, and as for poor Dido it
was not a willow in her hand with which she bade her
love to come again to Carthage, it was a sword on which
she impaled herself . . . poor poor Dido. It was there that
I read how the Egyptians were the first to master the art
of clairvoyance . . . they could by knowing the date of
a person's birth, tell the character, the life's eventualities,

and the day of death – but it was not called astrology, not until Roman times was it connected to the stars . . . but good lady you know all about that – those gods and goddesses had their seers . . . people just like you . . . they in their shrines and you in your painted caravan and I cannot tell you what a relief it is to be here . . . to be able to let off a little steam. Yes, it was bliss . . . the ever-changing light of the sea and no dusk . . . just daylight and then darkness . . . amorous dark, and when we came home it went on being bliss but life does stretch on, does it not, like a great yarn . . . and married people have to get to know one another's peculiarities . . . one another's habits . . . moods. Gerhardt was in the city in his chambers all week and then Fridays he drove home and the welcome, or should I say the host of welcomes, the two dogs, my wolfhound and his red setter, our little daft helper Aoife, and myself all rushing onto the drive, waving – Odysseus did not have such a welcome at Ithaca, far from it. A delicious dinner, roast with potato gratin, and apple fritters or charlotte russe for afters. Later, in the gloaming, we sat in the conservatory and discussed our week . . . the little highlights and the little lowlights, and he smoked a cigar and I would have a taste, yes a taste, more than a puff, and Mr Gentleman . . . well he knew so much . . . so much more than me and amazing how versatile even a cigar can be. Grand Marnier soufflé Sundays before he took off for the city . . . not a grass widow but a barrister's widow. For our holidays we never went abroad . . .

55

we sailed . . . we loved sailing and with a windfall from
a great aunt we bought a small houseboat and named it
after her – Violet Rose. We would set out from Athlone
and come all the way down along the Shannon, so beautiful, the breezes, the reeds, the quiet . . . endless prepara-
tions beforehand . . . rubber cushions, rugs . . . the primus
stove . . . methylated spirits . . . a first aid kit . . . straw
hats and rain hats . . . cream for the creepy crawlies . . .
scarcely speaking . . . just ambling along, and the smile,
the smiles . . . what a lovely thing a smile is . . . it speaks
multitudes. I lost two children very early on . . . he too
was cut up – 'there above the little grave, we kissed again
with tears.' Good lady, I confess, I am most afraid. Quite
by chance I came on it, a white shoebox, tucked into the
folds of a wide cedar that borders their fence and ours . . .
slippers . . . Cinderella slippers with rosebuds, concealed
in tissue paper . . . they were not my size . . . I have rather
large feet . . . the following morning they were gone . . .
someone had removed them. On that rare occasion, I did
tackle him, but he would not engage . . . said he wanted to
hear no more outlandish stories or delusions. It was in the
bedroom, in the very early morning . . . I feared for my
life. There are some moments, or perhaps they are mere
seconds, that stay in the deep freeze of the mind forever.
I might have dreamed it . . . I convinced myself for a time
that I did dream it . . . I said Millie, put it behind you . . .
you have been sleepwalking . . . you walked down the
avenue in your sleep. I got to be an ace fisherwoman on

our Shannon cruises . . . G couldn't believe it . . . he said it was something to do with not just the lightness but the swivel of my wrist. I was a tad unpopular with all the other fishing folk . . . a witch they called me. Of course at first I did not know how to play a fish, I rushed it and lost several . . . but Gerhardt schooled me and before long I excelled, I surpassed him. In the month of May, in the dapping season, we stayed out all day . . . all those millions of mayflies . . . the air scudded with them . . . Gerhardt said their courtship and their demise happened in the course of a single day . . . poor mayflies . . . nature's trick . . . poor mayflies . . . poor Dido. 'Never give all the heart outright' – Who said that? I have read that men have cycles just like us women . . . we have cycles because of the presence of the uterus – hence we are subject from time to time to hysteria – whereas men's cycles do not answer to the womb or the moon but to their own dastardly whims . . . they simply go on and off the creatures they call women. Of course anyone could have left the shoebox . . . any yokel or passer-by. Of late he stays out in the greenhouse till all hours . . . just like my father and his dog – my dog, I should say, Hector the fourth – yes Gerhardt stays there tending his vines, his cucumbers and his marrows which cross-pollinate . . . don't ask me how . . . he just places them side by side next to each other and somehow they cohabit . . . they breed . . . the saffron pollen wends its way to the opposite sex and . . . they propagate . . . .

He rarely falls in love . . . three times to my once and a half. A scandal occurred in his chambers in the Four Courts . . . one morning a junior happened to come in with a mound of papers and the secretary, a Miss O'Hanlaoin, was where she should not be and engaged in some hanky panky . . . fortunately it was hushed up . . . he did not feature half naked in a tabloid with his braces down, and moreover the junior was quite discreet, quite sterling. The overweening secretary not so. I found her notes in his pockets – demanding a showdown with me. Oh la la la la. It taught him a lesson. 'I will never leave you Millie . . . I will never leave you' was what he said. We went on a cruise for a reconciliation . . . some of the wives had at least twelve changes of attire . . . and the jewellery, so ostentatious, so unnecessary . . . we sat at the captain's table. I did get tiddly once or twice . . . the high heels and the ship's swaying did not help matters. When we docked for two days in a strange port, my husband played with children on the beach . . . a ball game – he and they tossed and kicked an orange ball . . . strangers' children . . . dusk-coloured children . . . certainly not white children, and they loved him. You see he has this aura – it emanates from him – by which people fall in love with him. They were seen – the buxom girl, the hussy, who has just left your caravan – they were seen one evening of late out on the lake and were caught in a squall . . . had to take shelter . . . something I learned as one does through the offices of a best friend. It was when

Dido and Aeneas took shelter that the fateful arrow of love struck. I do have one card up my sleeve, the most powerful card in the pack. One of our national poets, one of the triptych of Greats, has said that a young wife's, or for that matter, a young convent girl's trump card is the young cunt . . . but an older wife has a more powerful card . . . a darker card . . . one that we must not speak of. Are you with me, good lady . . . comprendé? I see you also do the tarot cards as well as the Crystal . . . I am familiar with some . . . the Hanged Man . . . La Tour . . . Temperance . . . The Scales of Justice. That hussy has no right to our gooseberries . . . none whatsoever . . . our apples . . . our crab apples . . . our pippins . . . our pears . . . our marrows . . . our redcurrants . . . our blackcurrants . . . our loganberries . . . our quinces . . . our greengages . . . our sugar plums . . . our medlars . . . our strawberries . . . our hops . . . our vines . . . our root vegetables . . . our harvests. Please, please. Open your door to me. I won't ask too much. I realise that it is a matter of some delicacy, of some discretion on your part . . . the Hippocratic oath or something akin to the priest in the confessional . . . you are bound to secrecy . . . all I ask is this. Being as you are a seer, what did you see? Have they gone in deep? By that I mean . . . you know what I mean. He's not old enough to be her father . . . he's old enough to be her grandfather . . . it is preposterous . . . it is absurd . . . it is, unthinkable . . . I think of Dido . . . I think of confit of duck in the fridge, since Sunday . . . I think of my husband's opal eyes and the card he wrote me last Christmas . . . 'twenty-two years and still my Queen' . . . I think I think I think. Good lady, open up . . . open your door . . . open your curtain . . . open it now . . . I cannot wait a second longer . . . do you understand . . . these louts are looking at me . . . they're laughing at me . . . the wild ponies are galloping . . . raising the dry dust in swarms. You are there. I know. I know it. I feel your presence in the non-rustle of the thick, dark-red lined curtain.

The journey hither takes three hours and thirty-five minutes, not allowing for mishaps. More than once, in our godforsaken part of the world, some wretch or beast has surrendered to the embraces of the rail track. Yes, the evening train winding and wending its way and all that fabled scenery and sky and skyline and torrents of rain.

Farewell dear callous lady.

*

Madame! There has been a strange development for which you are indirectly responsible. Had you seen me, it could not have occurred as I would have had to take the later train and not the six o'clock Express.

I had found an empty carriage and as the train gave its preliminary lurches, a door behind me, that I presumed led to the driver's cabin, was unlocked and a passenger ushered in. Even before I turned to look I knew, by the quickening of my pulse. It was not the footfall and not yet the voice, because no one had spoken; you could almost say my hunch was ethereal, yes, plucked from the ether. There was my husband, with his squashed briefcase, wedged under his elbow, and a stack of papers in his arms which he was holding awkwardly. He was flushed at having to race to catch the train.

'Millie,' he said, incredulous. As the train started his papers skived all about and he flopped onto the seat opposite and looked at me almost with wonder, as if he was seeing me in some way altered, his wife of twenty-two years leading a secret life, having a day up in Dublin, a rendezvous perhaps, and wearing a black cloche hat with a soft furry feather that tapered along the cheek.

'Where did we buy that hat?' he asked.

'We,' I said, lingering on the word, 'we bought it in Paris on the Rue du Dragon one Christmas Eve, as it began to snow.'

'So we did,' he said, and gazed into space as if he would have given anything to see falling snow.

The countryside, like our lives, is rolling by, stacks of chimney pots higgledy-piggledy, rooks and jackdaws whirling in the dusk of heaven, making that vast expanse their own.

In a while, he will lead me along to the dining car, a little agitation at the core of both our hearts, and we shall sit quietly, uncertain at what the future may hold.

Black Flower

'It's a dump,' Mona said.

'"Tis grand,' Shane said, looking around.

For an hour or more they had driven, under the prow of a range of mountain, in search of a restaurant that would be quiet but also cheerful, and now they had landed themselves in this big, gaunt room that seemingly served as both ballroom and dining room. A microphone on a metal stand took pride of place, and a bit of orange curtain lay crumpled on the bandstand, as if someone had flung it down there in petulance. One end of a long refectory table was covered with a white lace cloth under which there had been put a strip of red crêpe paper, and it was there they would most likely be seated.

It was late spring and when from the roadway they had spotted the rusted iron gates and the long winding avenue, they thought how suitable, and how enchanting it seemed. Moreover, the hotel had a lovely name – Glasheen. They drove up the long avenue, trees on either side, oak, sycamore, ash, all meshed together, fighting amiably as it were for ascendancy, and birds in their evening sallies, busier than the pigeons who cooed softly in their roomy roosts.

A battered jalopy with a 'For Sale' sign stood in the

car park that was separated from a nearby meadow by a rope of green cable. A sign on a post read 'Danger – High Voltage', and from a metal box there issued a burping, that every few seconds rose to a growl.

Close to the entrance was a butcher's van with the owner's name printed in tasteful brown lettering, and on the step a child's tractor filled with toy soldiers and wooden blocks. In the hallway, a nest of candles glimmered on a high whatnot and a luxurious flowering plant trailed and crept along the floor, amoeba-wise. The petals were a soft, velvety black, with tiny green eyes, pinpoints, and there was something both beautiful and sinister about it. She had never seen a black flower before. Since nobody answered, she went into an adjoining room, where a man had his face so close to the television screen he seemed to be conversing with it and took no notice of her. Two dogs dozed on a torn leather armchair. Presently, a girl came, a strapping young girl who could not say for certain if they did or did not do dinners, as the season was not yet in full swing. Nevertheless, she led the way to the gaunt, cheerless dining room.

They had driven so many miles, first to a town with a lake and a round tower, where they had strolled, then sat on dampish rough-hewn picnic stools and noted to each other how strange that others who had driven there had simply sat in their motor cars and stared out at the lake. He liked being with her, she could feel that. She didn't know him very well. She had volunteered to give

painting lessons in the prison in the Midlands, where he
was serving a long sentence. Though many came for the
first few classes, they eventually dropped away and by
the end, Shane was the only one. Sitting with his back
to her, finishing off a self-portrait, which was in viscous
gold and mustard yellows, she had asked him if he had
ever seen the paintings of Van Gogh, to which he said
he hadn't. She was reminded of Van Gogh because of
the upturned stump of a sneaker, on which the dry paint
bristled.

Walking in the graveyard beside the round tower,
she had asked very quietly, 'How do you find the world,
Shane?', since he was only out of prison a few short weeks.

'Crowded,' he had said, and half smiled.

While in prison, his wife had been shot, bathing their
child, shot in lieu of him and not long after, the child,
who was being reared with relatives, had also died, of
meningitis. On the evening that his wife had been shot,
he had gone to sleep while it was still bright, and though
the warders knocked and pounded on his cell door, to
tell him of it, he did not hear them. He reckoned that in
sleep he was postponing the news that he could not bear,
but would have to learn to bear. How he managed never
to crack up was a mystery to Mona.

A few days before Christmas, the governor of the prison had rung to tell her that there was a parcel left for her
in his office. It was the portrait wrapped in assorted carrier bags, and on the greeting card he had written, 'For

Mona . . . I'm sorry it's so crude.' Something about the message seemed unfinished, as if he had wanted to say more, and it was this hesitancy that emboldened her to ask if he would like to meet in Dublin, when he was let out. He was due out that spring, but it was kept a secret to avoid a media jamboree. She knew how reserved he was, he having mentioned that, though he ate in the refectory and played tennis three times a week, he kept to himself, and the best times were at night in the cell, listening to tapes of Irish music and songs. She imagined that on those nights he would mull on the past and on the future, too, possibly envisaging how the world had changed in the fifteen years since he was captured. It was a hair-raising capture that attracted the attention of the nation and confirmed him as a dangerous outlaw.

It so happened that he was released three days earlier than he had expected and she could scarcely believe it when he telephoned her in her studio in Dublin and said somewhat bashfully, 'It's me . . . I'm free.'

They had made an appointment to meet in a hotel, and standing on the steps on a crisp frosted morning, the winter boughs and branches in the park across the way jewelled in frost, she felt he was not coming, that something had prevented him. After almost an hour, a young boy in a braided outfit came and told her that she was wanted on the phone and brazenly repeated Shane's full name. He was in another hotel a mile away, and she told him, somewhat sternly, to wait there and not to budge.

Sitting with him in a booth of the second hotel, drinking tea, there was a tentativeness. It was strange to see him in a gaudy shirt and jeans, because in the prison Portakabin where she had visited him, everything was muted. Moreover, a policeman had always stood behind them, listening in, except for the odd time when he took a stroll, maybe to smoke a cigarette. They had not shook hands when they met on the steps of the hotel, but she knew by his way of looking at her that he was glad to see her and remarked on her hair being much nicer, loose like that. For the painting class it had always been tied back and made her look more severe.

'So you're free,' she said.

'I had only ten minutes' warning,' he said.

'How come?'

'The governor came down to the sewing room and said, "You have a car and a driver at your disposal for twenty-four hours, it'll take you anywhere you want."' As he said it, she remembered exactly having asked the governor if things would be all right for Shane when he got out.

As he spoke she recalled the shiver she had felt as the governor told her that there were many people who wished Shane dead.

'You mean the Brits?'

'Them and his own ... feuds ... feuds ... Put it this way, he'll always be a wanted man,' and he raised his arms to fend off questions.

'What were you sewing?' she asked, in surprise.

'Oh, bits and pieces for the lads . . . zips, darns, patches . . . there was a long queue.'

'Who taught you to sew?'

'We were ten children at home . . . the mother had a lot of other things to do,' he said shyly.

'So the lads will miss you?'

'They might,' he said, but without any show of emotion, then looking straight ahead he began to roll a cigarette, thoughtfully. He seemed then to be the very incarnation of loneliness, of isolatedness.

Some friends had pooled together to get him a second-hand motor car, and a few weeks later he suggested that they drive out into the country of an evening. It was agreed that she would travel by train and meet him in the town about eight miles north of Dublin, where he had found lodgings with a black woman, who chattered all day long to her humming birds and as he said did not ask questions.

Now they were in the big dining room, famished and waiting for the owner to come and tell them what she could possibly give them to eat. When she met Shane as arranged at the railway station, he was sitting against the outside wall eating an ice cream, and she wondered why a wanted man with a host of enemies would sit there, visible to all, in his new jeans and jazzy shirt.

His car was a little two-seater with a fawn coupe top. They had tried various restaurants along the way, to

no avail. In one, a sullen owner pulled the door barely
ajar and said there was no hope of teas as he was laid
up. Several times she got out of the car and went in,
only to discover that the restaurant was too rackety or
too dismal. She joked about these places when she got
back, described the tables, the lighting, the dried flowers
and so on, giving each place marks ranging from one to
ten. Shane didn't talk much, but he liked letting her talk.
The years inside had made him taciturn. Judging by the
newspaper photographs that had been taken on the day
he was captured, he had changed beyond recognition.
He had gone in, young and cavalier, and had come out
almost bald, with a thin rust moustache that somehow
looked as if it were spliced to his upper lip. He said once
to her and only once that she herself could be the judge
of his actions. He had fought for what he believed in,
which was for his country to be one, one land, one people
and not have a shank of it cut off.

When they came to the gateway leading to Glasheen,
she felt it was ideal, so sequestered and the building far
below, smothered in a grove of trees. Holding open one
half of the iron gate – she had put a stone to the other half
– she saw to one side a public telephone kiosk that looked
glaringly forlorn, the floor strewn with litter. The horse
chestnut trees were in full bloom, pink and white tassels
in a beautiful droop, and in the meadow lambs bleated
ceaselessly. It was pandemonium, what with them bleating and racing around for fear of losing their mothers.

'It's like a maternity ward,' Shane said and she wondered if he had ever been in one, as he was already in prison when his wife had given birth. Only his wife truly knew him and she was dead.

Looking at the stranded microphone, she said it was lucky they hadn't come on a dance night, as she was not a dancer.

'Me neither,' Shane said.

'Oh you'd dance if you were made to,' the owner said as she hurried in, drying her hands on a tea cloth, and told them about the lovely hunt ball they had had in the winter, people from all around, gentry and farmers and cattle dealers and highwaymen and God knows what.

'Are we bothering you?' Shane said.

'Aren't ye what I have been hoping for,' she said, and led them across to the long table that stretched almost to the window. When he sat down he smiled. It was the way he smiled that drew people to him, and the owner, quick to recognise it, introduced herself as Wynne and said proudly that they were in luck because her good-for-nothing husband had caught a salmon and she would poach it, along with potatoes and cabbage. Meanwhile, she said, they should tuck into the drink and she would bring bread to mop it up. There was a slight hitch, as she was inexpert at opening the bottle of wine, which Mona had already ordered. The corkscrew buckled and bits of crumpled cork floated in the pale amber liquid.

'Just enjoy the view and the rolling countryside,' Wynne said, and sallied off muttering what a nice man Shane was and what nice manners and how manners maketh man.

'This is nice,' he said. He liked the wine, though he was not used to it. She could tell he was not used to it because his eyes became a little foggy, like steam on a kitchen window when pots are boiling over. They could hear Wynne talking to the dozy girl in the kitchen, as their arrival had created a little flurry.

'Your eyes are the colour of tobacco,' Mona said.

'Is that good or bad?' he asked.

'It's good, ' she said.

Turning to Wynne, who had just come in with a loaf of bread, he asked what the room rates were for the night.

'We could negotiate that,' Wynne said, and winked as she toddled off.

'You're not thinking of staying in this dungeon,' Mona said.

'No one would find me here,' he said, gravely.

'Where will you live Shane?'

'Maybe in the west,' he said, but vaguely. She pictured him in some cold, isolated cottage, by himself, wrapped in an overcoat, on edge, day and night on the look-out.

'Do you worry about . . . about reprisals?' she asked.

'I'd be worried for others,' he said, and looked at her with such concern, such tenderness, across the reaches of the wide table, the flames from the stout candle guttering in the breeze from the open window, half his face in shadow.

'Do you think you'll go back to . . .'

'The fight isn't over . . . isn't done,' he said grimly.

She didn't ask anything further. There were always distances between them, a part of him cut off from her and from everyone, a remoteness. How different the two hims, the young invincible buccaneer and the man sitting opposite her, ageing and dredged, his deeds locked inside him.

'It's alright,' she said, not even sure of what she was saying.

'It is,' he answered, also unsure.

The poached salmon was a sturdy lump from which the head and tail had been cursorily lopped. The skin, hanging in a long shred, looked like fly paper, and though the outside was cooked nicely, the inside was rawish and around the bone the juices were a pale blood colour. Wynne hacked it jubilantly with an old carving knife and conveyed pieces onto Shane's plate with bravado. She then picked up the hot boiled potatoes with her bare hands and filled his plate in her desire to please him. Mona asked for a smaller portion as Shane apologised for the mound he had been given.

'There'll be jelly and custard, so leave a gap,' Wynne said and went off proudly, humming.

Very soon after, he listened as if he had heard something that was no longer the bleating lambs, because in the fading light they had gone quieter.

'What?' Mona asked.

'Car.'

The car drove in at hectic speed, lights fully on and then drove off again, with a vengeance.

'Ah, youngsters, hoping there was a disco,' Wynne said, having come back in with the white sauce for the salmon. But he was not listening to her, he was only listening now to his own thoughts and his appetite had gone. He drank a few more swigs of wine and jumped up.

'Toilet,' he said and reached out and touched her sleeve. She watched him go, something so wounded about him, his clothes clinging to his thin body, his sleeves rolled up as he tugged at the loose door knob. Then peculiarly, he ran back and took his jacket off the back of the chair.

Since he was away for quite a while, Wynne, who had been coming in and out, brought an old dented cloche to put over his dinner, as both of them watched through the open door into the dark passageway. The two dogs, so inert a short while previous, raised an ongoing terrible howl, as if catastrophe was about to befall the house. Wynne said it portended thunder, as they never yelped at visitors, not even at tradesmen, but the onset of thunder always sent them crazy. She predicted that presently there would be flashes of lightning, the grounds and the meadow intermittently lit up. They waited, but the summer lightning did not come.

'I wonder what's keeping him,' Wynne said.

'He's not used to drink,' Mona said quietly.

'Lovely man . . . lovely smile,' Wynne said, and again looked, expecting him to appear, in that quick, stealth-like way of his.

At length, Wynne said, 'Do you think I should get Jack to go and investigate?'

They had left the dining room and were in the hall-way facing the door that said Gents, with the metal 'G' askew on a loose rusted nail. Mona thought how awful if he had passed out and how ashamed he would be. Jack was summoned from where he was stationed, close up to the television screen, and rising he muttered something, then went into the Gents and closed the door behind him. Soon Wynne pushed it in so that they could be of assistance.

'He's not here,' Jack called.

'Where is he then?' Wynne shouted.

'He went out . . . he got change for the pay phone,' Jack said and instantly she guessed that he had gone to phone one of his comrades to come for her, as he would have to disappear.

The dogs were already on the avenue, running back and forth in a froth, and ready to tear anyone to pieces.

Both women ran and Jack followed behind, calling after them.

People stood on the far side of the gate, muted and in shock. Shane lay half in and half out of the telephone kiosk, his eyes, his tobacco-coloured eyes, still open, staring up at the sky with its few isolated stars. He was gasping to say something, but the strength had almost left him. He could not say what he most wanted to say. The onlookers stood in a huddle, baffled, not knowing who they were looking at, or why he had been slain, while simply making a telephone call. The guards had already been called, and one woman, who had been first on the scene, said she had heard him repeatedly utter, 'Oh Jesus, oh Mary,' but her companion stoutly contradicted that. Mona wanted to kneel by him and shut his eyes, but she was too afraid to stir. If only someone would shut his eyes, but she dared not, for fear of them. He looked so desolate and so unbefriended, the breath just ebbing away and the instant it left him, she let out a terrible cry. He was dead. Dead for a cause that others did not believe in, and as if on cue a youth who had been going by, stopped, dismounted his black brutish motorcycle, threw down his helmet, and crossed with the officiousness of a pallbearer. Looking down at the corpse, he recognised Shane and repeated his name with evident outrage and disgust. He seemed almost ready to kick him. The group recoiled, stricken, not only with fear, but with revulsion. The brief spate of pity had turned ugly. Wynne shrieked at Mona – 'A murderer . . . you brought a murderer under my roof where my grandchildren slept,' and then lunged fiercely, as Jack caught her, repeating the same phrase over and over again, 'It's all right . . . it's all right . . . he's history now . . . he can't harm us anymore.'

The police cars had arrived and big burly men, in a lather of curiosity and vindication, hurried to look at the assassin, in whose bloodied death, they rejoiced.

'What goes around comes around,' one said with a smugness.

Those that had been first on the scene were told to drive to the police station in the town, while Jack, Wynne, and Mona were ordered back to the hotel for interrogation.

Jack and Wynne hurried on, as the dopey girl and a boy came to meet them, clinging to one another for protection. Mona lagged behind, dreading their questions and their abhorrence of her. It had begun to drizzle. A brooding quiet filled the entire landscape and the trees drank in the moisture. There would be another death to undo his and still another and another in the long grim chain of reprisals. Hard to think that in the valleys murder lurked, as from the meadow there came not even a murmur, the lambs in their foetal sleep, innocent of slaughter.

Plunder

One morning we wakened to find that there was no border – we had been annexed to the fatherland. Of course
we did not hear of it straightaway as we live in the wilds,
but a workman who comes to gather wood and fallen
boughs told us that soldiers had swarmed the town and
occupied the one hotel. He said they drank there, got
paralytic, demanded lavish suppers, and terrorised the
maids. The townspeople hid, not knowing which to fear
most, the rampaging soldiers or their huge dogs that ran
loose without muzzles. He said they had a device for
examining the underneath of cars – a mirror on wheels
to save themselves the inconvenience of stooping. They
were lazy bastards.

The morning we sighted one of them by the broken
wall in the back avenue we had reason to shudder. His
camouflage was perfect, green and khaki and brown, the
very colours of this mucky landscape. Why they should
come to these parts baffled us and we were sure that very
soon they would scoot it. Our mother herded us all into
one bedroom, believing we would be safer that way –
there would be no danger of one of us straying and we
could keep turns at the watch. As luck had it, only the
week before we had gathered nuts and apples and stored

them on wooden trays for the winter. Our mother worried about our cow, said that by not being milked her poor udder would be pierced with pain, said the milk would drip all over the grass. We could have used that cow's milk. Our father was not here, our father had disappeared long before.

On the third morning they came and shouted our mother's name – Rosanna. It sounded different, pronounced in their tongue, and we wondered how they knew it. They were utter hooligans. Two of them roughed her out, and the elder tugged on the long plait of her hair.

Our mother embraced each of us and said she would be back presently. She was not. We waited, and after a fearful interval we tiptoed downstairs but could not gain entry to the kitchen because the door between it and the hall was barricaded with stacked chairs. Eventually we forced our way through, and the sight was grisly. Her apron, her clothes, and her underclothes were strewn all over the floor, and so were hairpins and her two side combs. An old motorcar seat was raised onto a wooden trough in which long ago she used to put the feed for hens and chickens. We looked in vain through the window, thinking we might see her in the back avenue or better still coming up the path, shattered, but restored to us. There was one soldier down there, his rifle cocked. Where was she? What had they done to her? When would she be back? The strange thing is that none of

us cried and none of us broke down. With a bit of effort
we carried the stinking car seat out and threw it down
the three steps that led from the back door. It was all we
could do to defy our enemies. Then we went up to the
room and waited. Our cow had stopped moaning, and
we realised that she too had been taken and most likely
slaughtered. The empty field was ghost-like, despite the
crows and jackdaws making their usual commotion at
evening time. We could guess the hours roughly by the
changing light and changing sky. Later the placid moon
looked in on us. We thought, if only the workman would
come back and give us news. The sound of his chainsaw
used to jar on us, but now we would have welcomed it as
it meant a return to the old times, the safe times, before
our mother and our cow were taken. Our brother's
wooden flute lay in the fire grate, as he had not the heart
to play a tune, even though we begged for it.

On the fifth morning we found some reason to jubi-
late. The sentry was gone from his post, and no one came
to stand behind that bit of broken wall. We read this as
deliverance. Our mother would come back. We spoke of
things that we would do for her. We got her clean clothes
out of the wardrobe and lay them neatly on the bed. Her
lisle stockings hanging down, shimmered pink in a shaft
of sunlight, and we could imagine her legs inside them.
We told each other that the worst was over. We bit on
apples and pelted each other with the butts for fun. Our
teeth cracked with a vengeance on the hazelnuts and the

walnuts, and picking out the tasty, fleshy particles, we shared them with one another like true friends, like true family. Our brother played a tune. It was about the sun setting on a place called 'Boulevouge'.

Our buoyancy was shortlived. By evening we heard gunshot again, and a soldier had returned to the broken bit of wall, a shadowy presence. Sleep was impossible and so we watched and we prayed. We did that for two whole days and nights, and what with not eating and not sleeping, our nerves got the better of us and, becoming hysterical, we had to slap each other's faces, slap them smartly, to bring common sense into that room.

The hooligans in their camouflage have returned. They have come by a back route, through the dense woods and not up the front avenue as we expected.

They are in the kitchen, laughing and shouting in their barbarous tongues. Fear starts to seep out of us, like blood seeping. If we are taken all together, we might muster some courage, but from the previous evidence it is likely that we will be taken separately. We stand, each in our corner, mute, petrified, like little effigies, our eyes fastened to the knob of the door, our ears straining beyond it, to gauge which step of stairs they are already stomping on.

How beautiful it would be if one of us could step forward and volunteer to become the warrior for the others. What a firmament of love ours would be.

A deathly emptiness to the whole world, to the fields
and the sacked farmyards and the tumbledown shacks.
Not a soul in sight. Not an animal. Not a bird. Here
and there mauled carcasses and bits of torn skins where
animals must have fought each other in their last frenzied hungers. I almost got away. I was walking towards
somewhere that I didn't know, somewhere safe. There
had been no soldiers for weeks. They'd killed each other
off. It was hard to know which side was which, because
they swapped sides the way they swapped uniforms. My
mother and later my brother and my two sisters had
been taken. I was out foraging and when I came back
our house was a hulk of smoke. Black ugly smoke. I only
had the clothes I stood up in, a streelish green dress and
a fur coat that was given to my mother once. It used to
keep us warm in bed, and sometimes when it slipped
onto the floor I would get out to pick it up. It felt luxurious, the hairs soft and tickling on bare feet. That was the
old world, the other world, before the barbarians came.
Why they came here at all is a mystery, as there was no
booty, no gold mines, no silver mines – only the woods,
the tangly woods, and in some parts tillage, small patches
of oats or barley. Even to think of corn, first green and
then a ripening yellow, or the rows of cabbage, or any
growing thing, was pure heartbreak. Maybe my brother
and sisters are across the border or maybe they are dead.
I moved at dusk and early night, bunched inside the
fur coat. I wanted to look old, to look a hag. They did

not fancy the older women; they wanted young wom-
en and the younger the better, like wild strawberries. It
was crossing a field that I heard the sound of a vehicle,
and I ran, not knowing there was such swiftness in me.
They were coming, nearer and nearer, the wheels slurping over the ridged earth that bordered the wood that
I was heading into. The one who jumped out picked
me up and tossed me to the Head Man. They spluttered
with glee. He sat me on his lap, wedged my mouth open,
wanting me to say swear words back to him. His eyes
were hard as steel and the whites a yellowy gristle. Their
faces were daubed with paint and they all had puce
tattoos. The one that drove was called Gypsy. That drive
was frantic. Me screaming, screaming, and the Head
Man slapping me like mad and opening me up as though
I was a mess of potage. They stopped at a disused lime
kiln. He was first. When he splayed me apart I thought
I was dead, except that I wasn't. You don't die when you
think you do. The subordinates used their hands as stir-
rups. When I was turned over I bit on the cold lime floor
to clean my mouth of them. Their shouts, their weight,
their tongues, their slobber, the way they bore through
me, wanting to get up into my head, to the God parti-
cle. That's what an old woman in the village used to call
it, that last cranny where you say prayers and confide in
yourself the truth of what you feel about everything and
everyone. They couldn't get to it. I had stopped screaming. The screams were stifled. Through the open roof I

saw a buzzard glide in a universe of blue. It was waiting for another to be with it, and after a time that other came that was its comrade and they glided off into
those crystalline nether-reaches. Putting on their trousers, they kept telling each other to hurry the fuck up.
The Head Man stood above me, straddled, the fur coat
over his shoulders, and he looked spiteful, angry. The
blood was pouring out of me and the ground beneath
was warm. I saw him through the slit in my nearly shut
eyes. For a minute I thought he might kill me and then
he turned away as if it wasn't worth the bother, the mess.
The engine had already started when Gypsy ran back
and placed a cigarette across my upper lip. I expect he
was trying to tell me something. As children we were
told that why we have a dent in our upper lip is because
when we are born an angel comes and places a forefinger there for silence, for secrecy. By degrees I came back.
Little things, the air sidling through that small clammy
enclosure and the blood drying on me, like resin. Long
ago, we had an aluminium alarm clock with the back
fallen off, that worked on a single battery, but batteries
were scarce. Our mother would take out the battery and
we'd guess the time by the failing light, by the dusk, by
the cockcrow and the one cow, the one faithful cow that
stood, lowing, at the paling, waiting to be milked. One
of us would go out with a bucket and the milking stool.
When she put the battery back the silver needle would
start up and then the two hands, like two soft black

insects, crept over each other in their faithful circuit. The lime-green dress that I clung to, that I clutched, that I dug my fingernails into, is splotched with flowers, blood-red and prodigal, like poppies. Soon as I can walk I will set out. To find another, like me. We will recognise each other by the rosary of poppies and the speech of our eyes. We, the defiled ones, in our thousands, scattered, trudging over the land, the petrified land, in search of a safe haven, if such a place exists.

Many and terrible are the roads to home.

Inner Cowboy

Flat, watery land. Big lakes, little lakes, turloughs that
filled up in the rain and rivers a reddish brown from the
iron in the soil. Curly didn't pay much heed to scenery,
he was used to it. But he did notice the mist through the
window when he got up early, everything blurry, the
pots and the wheelbarrows in the backyard, the magpies
lined up on the chimney stacks, and the cat, pleased with
herself after her fill of mice and bats in the night – black
night people called it. That cat was run over and got
renamed 'Lucky to be alive' and had a ridge in her tail,
like a ponytail. Felim, Curly's boss, collected him every
morning and brought him to the hardware shop, in the
other town, eight miles away. Riding along, he'd see the
mist lift and it was like seeing a grand lady lifting the veil
of her hat, gradual, gradual, but he did not say so to his
boss or he'd be jeered at.

He disliked his boss. *I dislike this man* he'd say, sitting
as far apart from him as he possibly could. Curly often
confabbed with himself in private.

He had a brown shop coat, even though he wasn't
let serve customers. All day he was hauling things back
and forth from the store room, across the yard, over the
puddles, crates of paint and filler and wallpaper and lino

and mats and carpeting and buckets and bundles of kindling. There was a big high counter of cherry wood and, behind it, loads of drawers for nuts and bolts and nails, which Curly had to keep tidy, because things got jumbled. Felim was pure ignorant towards him and once went so far as to call him a 'retard' in front of customers. He was vexed, but he swallowed his pride, because he needed the wages for the rent of his room. The council paid some and he had to pay the rest. When Felim got the hump or had a hangover he kicked all before him and one day he kicked Curly in the shins. He could sue him for that, but he was too afraid of the guards.

The singing in the choir was what kept him going. They learned the words from a big songbook that took three pairs of hands to hold. Miss Boyce played the piano and conducted the choir. She was a lady. She would make an apple cake and bring it in and give it round. Then she got an infection, was out for a month, and after she came back she slid off the piano stool and fell. She died in a week. They sang for her in the church, sang with all their might – 'Here I am Lord, Lord of the sea and sky.'

He kissed her in the coffin before they put the lid on it. The other person he kissed was a nun kneeling in the grotto, because she looked sad. They were the two people, apart from his granny, that he kissed. He didn't remember his mother because she died when he was young and his father scooted. *No, there is no romance in my life and that is something I miss*, he would say to himself, believing that it would come, that it was like a little mustard seed and would grow. His granny said he was the best person alive and that made him feel great and not a retard.

His granny loved the olden days, when shops were drapery and grocery and hardware all in one. At the town square on a fair day, every Christmas, she sold her turkeys and was still calling her turkeys back. After she lost her husband and was all alone she got a pattern book and crocheted a beautiful white bed shawl. That kept her alive. But she wasn't as clued up as she used to be and dozed a lot in the chair and came awake always saying the same thing, 'Oh Curly, you asked for a biscuit and Coca Cola and I gone and got you a biscuit and a glass of milk.'

Curly preferred the bog to the quarries. The quarries were big ugly places, cross places and noisy, flying dust everywhere, showers of it black and gritty, from all the crushing and the blasting. The bogs were more peaceful, stretching to the horizon, a dun brown, with cushions of moss and spagunam and the cut turf in little stooks, igloos, with the wind whistling through them, drying them out. The birds flew high up in the air, only came down at night to feed and to suck. At school, the master read from an encyclopedia that bogs were a place to bury butter, to take a shortcut, and to dispose of a murdered one. Curly helped in the bog in the summer, because even though turf was cut with machinery it still needed humans to lay it and foot it and bag it and bring it home.

One day his friend Roddy wanted to be alone with his girlfriend and he got Curly up on the tractor, put it in first gear, and said, 'Take your boot off the brake and 'twill go.' And he did. And he was driving all over the place, slurping and lurching, the wheels sunk in the mire and he rollicking about, like he did in the dodgem cars at the carnival. Ever after in his dreams he was behind the wheel, powerful. When he got on Roddy's red Honda, that was different, that was trouble. Big time. Only a few hundred yards down a country road and didn't a squad car drive up and he was stopped and questioned, asked for his driving licence and insurance. He had neither. After ten days he received the summonses, one for not having the said documents and the second for failing to produce them. That day in the local district court, he wore a white baseball cap and made sure to address the judge as Judge. The reason he gave for speeding was because of the carburettor – said it would blow out if he went any slower, that he had to open her up for a mile or so. The judge was furious, boomed that he did not tolerate balderdash and called Curly a *brazen ingrate*. On a document, he was listed as P.O.A., which meant some kind of offender.

A crowd went to the races at Cheltenham in England and, feeling left out, he said to himself, *Curly, why don't you do something really wild.* He had a twenty-pound note and at lunch break he went down to the bookies, looked up numbers, and just went for number thirty-seven. Just like that. He watched the race in the hardware shop, in between doing things, and saw that his horse didn't fall, but didn't see the finish. When he went back to the book-ies, Tilda asked him was he going out that night and he said he was skint and then she told him to go down into the little reception area and help himself to hot chocolate from the machine. When she came a bit later, there was a couple there and she said, 'Give a guess what this young man has won,' and they couldn't and neither could he. Oh, she teased it out, saying what a lucky lad he was and he'd be going places. Then she whispered in his ear, his horse had come in at fifty to one. He was flabbergasted. She gave him the money in the back room. It was one thousand pounds in different notes. He had been invited to a twenty-first that night and treated himself to a new suit, a striped suit, and got a radiator for his granny, one with the dial high up so she didn't have to bend, and a pink feather boa for Tara, the birthday girl. He had his hair cut and then spiked with gel. The life and soul of the party, everybody congratulating him and saying they'd all go to a match in Dublin, make a weekend of it. He sang the song that he always sang – 'The Walk-ing Man I Am.' With the rest of the money he bought a black mare that turned out to be very bold, but she'd have a foal and he could sell it. The mare was in one of Donie's fields. Donie lived in the next county and was a third cousin of the family.

*

Every third Saturday Curly worked for Mrs Mulkearns, who ran a bed and breakfast. He put horse manure around a belt of young trees – maples, pines, and birches that were planted up near the main road to muffle the sound of the passing cars and lorries. Conor was the gardener, always muttering to himself. He said rich bastards were ruining Ireland, poisoning it, the McSorley brothers and their ilk grabbing, buying up every perch of farm, bog, and quarry they could get their hands on. Hadn't they destroyed a sacred wood with its yew trees, bulldozed it, in order to make pasture to fatten livestock. With the mist vanishing, Conor would point to the last wisps of dew on the palings and on the posts, like diamonds, zillions of diamonds. If only they could catch them, they'd be as rich as the McSorleys.

Mrs Mulkearns did something gorgeous. She invited him and his granny to come and stay for a night. It was like going abroad. They got there at dusk. Being autumn, the trees up along the avenue were all sorts of plum colours and there were still flowers in the flowerbeds and in the hallway a tall clock in a glass-fronted case and the polished pendulums, solid as truncheons. There was a big fire in the room, pictures on every inch of wall, and books and ornaments and a second clock on the mantelpiece ticking. Mrs Mulkearns carried in a tray with sandwiches, scones, a variety of jams, and a cake, and she sat with them and explained the different flavours in the jams and how she came upon the Austrian recipe for the cake, which was shaped like a log and had a soft white butter icing. It was called a Stollen, from an old Prussian name that meant 'awaken'. All of a sudden she decided to tell a story of her youth, her harum scarum youth. She was in a convent and, with two other girls, plotted to get over the stone wall to meet two boys and walk three miles out of the town, to look at a haunted house. It was creepy, them just pushing the door in and every stick of furniture still in the rooms, and in the music room, a piano, sheet music strewn all over, and a beeswax candle in a brass holder – the very same as if the dead owner was about to come in. When they heard footfalls they ran and ran, and she and the two girls were expelled from the convent. His granny began a story but lost the thread of it and then it was his turn and he told about going to the bookies and picking number thirty-seven, but he did not tell what had transpired between him and Donie.

Lying in the strange four-poster, he thought on the matter and said, *Awaken Curly, awaken.* There was things in the media every single day about the haul from the notorious bank robbery in the north – how some traceable notes were retrieved, more found in chimneys and broom cupboards, and there were warrants for people whom the state intended to call. He might be one of those people. One evening, at closing time, Donie called to the shop and brought him across to the chipper, where he had his favourite things, chips with prawn sauce and grated cheese and mince. Donie wanted a favour, he wanted something hidden. A bag. He said Curly was not to worry, as he would not do anything to harm him or his granny and that it was only temporary. It could go in the granny's shed. That shed beat all for clutter. There was stuff in it going back hundreds of years, an old sidecar with a trap wedged over it, milk churns, milk tankards, breast slanes and foot slanes from when turf was cut by hand, and fenders and picture frames and old chairs and a horsehair sofa with the leather slashed and the coarse hair spilling out. There was a hole in the floor under the sidecar, where his great-grandfather hid his pike in Fenian times and his grandfather hid the bottles of potcheen and where he would hide the bag. Donie said there would be a reward and he asked what and Donie said, 'Name your poison', and he did. He wanted a mobile phone and straight away, when they'd finished the tea, they went to the phone shop, where there were hundreds and hundreds of phones all standing up, like little soldiers, waiting to be claimed. He picked a pink one, light pink, the colour of cake icing, and next day people at work were gaping at it and touching it, mad jealous. He put three telephone numbers into the memory, his granny's, Donie's, and his boss. He put the boss's number in because he longed for the morning that he could ring up and say, *I'm not coming in today, Mutt, and I'm not coming in ever*. He longed for that day.

The money was in a black plastic bag inside a hold-all, and feeling it in his bedroom that first night he wondered how many thousands were in it, because he knew it was money, it wasn't anything else. He placed it on the floor of the wardrobe, laid it into his jacket and tied the buttons so that it looked like a dead person, a dead person with the legs sawn off. Then he put the baseball cap on it. If anyone came into that room and opened the wardrobe, they'd get a fright, but no one would.

It is winter evening and the men in the quarry are already knocking off. But in Mr McSorley's office there is uproar, as Daragh McSorley himself thunders at Seamus the foreman, who stands mute, lank and unable to control the shaking.

'Tell me more Seamus . . . moremore . . . it's music to my ears, it's Beethoven and Boyzone and Glenstall Monks rolled into one,' and before Seamus can even attempt to answer, McSorley is yelling what he has already been told, what he has already ingested – Hanrahan, a fucking eejit, a fucking moron, on his mobile, not thinking, rams his digger straight into the tank of diesel and, presto, thousands of litres have spewed onto the rained-on yard, making those rainbow colours so beloved of youngsters – said diesel already flowing through the porous limestone down to the river and onwards to the estate of houses in the valley below. Forty fucking families who hate his guts are now alerted to a peculiar smell in their kitchen and weird patches of damp seeping up through their foundations. Forty families baying at the gates; the Gardai, the council, the fisheries board all on his back, his quarry shut down indefinitely, loaders, crushers, lying idle, men laid off, bank repayments to the tune of fifty grand a month. Marvellous, inspirational, a whammy, a catastrophic environmental and human fuckup. At that, he reaches for his calculator and with instantaneous lucidity begins to tot up the gargantuan sums about to be lost.

Seamus watches the savage snarling expression, not yet knowing how long it will take for the spree of rage to subside, but guessing the finale – McSorley tearing wads of newspaper to chew, then spit out, because his anger can no longer be contained in a violent welter of words.

'Hanrahan is very sorry . . . he was ringing the hospital to inquire about his mother and getting no answer,' Seamus said, only to be silenced, because McSorley does not give a tinker's curse if Walter Mitty and Walter Mitty's ailing mother are dead in a ditch. The tank has got to be removed and a cleanup operation commenced at once.

'It can't be done tonight,' Seamus says.

'Can't! Can't!' McSorley roars. Can't is a verb he does not tolerate. Can't does not close a deal. There are no prizes for can't. Can't is the breast that losers are suckled on. That tank goes and is replaced with an identical one, all surface evidence is erased, stones taken up, crushed, buried, and clean unsmelling stone put in their place.

Alone, he drops down into his chair, drenched in sweat, and spits out the last gob of wet newspaper, then reaches into his bottom drawer for the brandy and his pewter mug. The first slug he drinks direct from the bottle and studies his reflection in the mug, his mouth foaming, his features distended. He does not like what he sees, because he is a vain man, proud of his jutting jaw, his mineral-blue eyes, his ramrod posture, and the cropped tawny mustache that singles him out from the lubbers and jobbers all around. He asks himself, 'Who am I, what am I' and answers 'I am Daragh McSorley, from the big house on the hill' – lawns, topiary, sculptures the size of cannon, a fragrant wife, Kitty, panelled walls, priceless paintings, a library of first editions, a yacht named after his daughter bobbing in the wintry waters off the coast of Spain, and a family to assuage his every mood, his bursts of temper, a devoted family that is his pride and joy.

But no one really knows him as he is, no one knows the scope of his ambition, the passion, the relentless unrest. Only Dr Tubridy got a glimpse of it once – Tubridy, aping the English mores with his tweeds and his trilby hat, put it to him in the surgery, after the second by-pass – asked him what made him tick.

'Lust,' he answered.

'For the fair sex,' Tubridy said.

'For everything . . . Medbh the Connaught Queen, has nothing on me, with her avarice for dominions, herds, jewels and booty.'

'And thy fellow man?' Tubridy put it to him.

'A cheque book speaks louder than the act of perfect contrition,' he answered and laughed, and Tubridy laughed with him, but nervously.

He was famous for his loud laugh that had little mirth in it. It confused people, it kept them dangling. As for bad feeling, there was so much bad feeling vented on him that he could bottle it and sell it like holy water. His wife, Kitty, mortified that Sunday after mass, when a mad eejit of a woman who had done upholstery for a block of houses, came up to him cursing and screaming, 'You broke me, you broke me, Mr McSorley,' and he not losing the cool one bit, giving her the big smile and assuring her that it would be looked into. Soon she was timorous, almost apologetic, and he walked tall to the car, Kitty pinching him and asking, 'In the name of God Daragh, in the name of God, what did you do?' It wasn't long after that that the stone eagles were hacked off the piers of his front gates and dogs were set on Kitty when she was out for a walk.

Another thing, never in his cups did he luxuriate in that maudlin stuff about hunger and privation. He knew it in his marrow. Lesser men than him would go on about crubeens and a turnip for Christmas dinner, or a grandmother pulled off her bicycle when she was taking the salmon that her man had poached from the river, to sell to the fishmonger in the town, taken down off her bicycle and brought to the county jail.

'Be absolute in your aim' was what he told himself

while he was still in short trousers. On the day when he hired his first lorry and trusted that guiding star that led him through mountain gorges to his Eldoraldo, a disused quarry. He got out, looked at a sheer wall of rock over two hundred feet high, and imagined the wealth that lay hidden within the belly of it.

It is Friday night, the night he and Kitty – along with Ambrose, his brother and partner, and Ambrose's wife, Isolde, the ex-beauty queen – will go up the country to a simple olde worlde pub for dinner. It's his way of letting it be known that he hasn't lost touch with his roots and, moreover, they have taken on a young chef who had just got his degree in Switzerland. Walking to his car after work, the jacket over his shoulder, he can see the men, the few trusted ones breaking the stones with their jackhammers. Lights gleamed in the valley down below, and from a hillside farmstead comes the sound of a cow in labour. He knew that sound. Sometimes the memory of it took him unawares, that low grieving sound of a cow in labour, but instantly he shut it out. Such things belonged to his former and unhardened self. He is no longer that man. He is a man frequently described in the newspapers as ruthless and with a criminal coldness.

Yes, it's their evening for up-the-country, and Isolde, with her range of accessories – because she's an accessory freak, in the black gloves with sequins – raving about too much dairy in her diet, too much frigging Krug in her diet, not like his little Kitty, one gin and tonic that she nurses faithfully, because she read somewhere that Winston Churchill always nursed his drink. Isolde falling not once, not twice, but thrice at their barbecue at the end of summer, whereas his little Kitty is up with the lark, morning Mass, a bit of baking, her prize herb garden and a brisk walk in the afternoon to keep her figure. Chalk and cheese, Kitty and Isolde, like Daragh and Ambrose, quiet and staid, brothers yoked together, in their crooked deeds and their crooked deals. Kitty knew how to keep her man, that lady journalist sashaying up to him at the function in Dublin, to ask how she could get in touch so as to raise his profile, stressing his works for charity and his role as a family man, and Kitty answering from the far end of the festive table, 'Through me, through me.'

Next day Curly was a hero. The words ran away with him, boasting how he had pulled a calf from its mother, up there on Pat-the-Bonham's bit of land, Pat having gone to Lourdes as a volunteer, when lo and behold, up there in the silence and the gloom there was this hullabaloo from down in the quarry below, security lights turned off and he reckoning that it was some gang stealing diesel or stealing stones. Then, as he told it, the cow got very agitated, running around in circles, and the noise was atrocious, a drilling sound, a zzzzzzzzzzz, like from the key-cutting machine in the shop, only louder,

and then the claps of metal hitting other metal and echo-
ing back, so that the cow bolted from the building and
ran off. He followed, but each time she got away, over
grass and thicket, he demented, in case she got caught in
a crevice of the ravine, or that the calf would slip out and
split its head on rock or bits of drainage pipe embedded
in the earth. When he got to the moment when he knew
he would have to deliver a calf, he asked them, his listen-
ers, to just picture it – he with only a small torch and not
a bit of rope or twine, seeing the forelegs jutting out, but
not able to catch them because of their being so slimy,
and doing the only thing he could think of, which was
to take off his sweater, get a grip on them, and pull and
pull, until the calf came out in a big plop on the damp
ground and he, as he said, roared with joy and relief.
Then nature took its course, the mother licked the sac,
took her time over it, licked the crusted eyelids, chewed
the cord, and the calf began its pathetic attempts to get
up, the mother unable to do that for it, only the calf itself
could do that, and eventually, staggering on its little legs
and going straight to the udder.

'*Euphoria*' was the only word Curly could find to
describe what he felt.

By nightfall, as he told it in the chipper, the pitch black
was blacker, the noise from the quarry suspicious, but
worst of all, the birth was complicated, as one of the calf's
feet was folded back inside the mother and he who knew
nothing about veterinary had to put his hand in, jiggle it

around to get it forward and enable the calf to slide out, which it did.

The *euphoria* would be short lived.

Over the next days, the environmental agency was flooded with complaints, some in person and some by phone, families up there, irate at the fact that their water was contaminated, that smears of greasy film appeared in their sinks and on their baths, and the springs that fed the reservoir had lagoons of oil floating upon them. Men were called to monitor the damage, and when fish were found dead in the river an enquiry was set up as to what might have caused such spillage, though those up there already knew that it had only come from one place, the detested quarry.

It was the tapping on the window at night that Curly came to dread and he being called out. First it was Seamus the foreman, telling him that he would have to comply, otherwise the McSorleys would punish him. Then it was Ambrose, saying that they knew he had made a statement to the Guards, but that he would have to retract it. He could say that he saw nothing and that he heard nothing and that anyhow, he had bad sight. The proof that he had bad sight they had already ascertained, because of the many pairs of glasses Curly had been prescribed down the years. Finally, it was Daragh McSorley himself, just dropping by for a friendly chat, asked who was his favourite pop group, when last had he been to Galway, and how was his granny doing on her lonesome out there in the wilds. Then he said that Curly had nothing to worry about, all he had to do was stand up in the court and say he had made up a story to keep himself company out there on the lonely mountainside. Muldoon, a friendly solicitor, would help, coach him and put him through his paces. If he played ball and the case was quashed, Santa would come and Santa would come to his granny also and to tell her that. Curly looked at Mr McSorley's big tall frame silhouetted against the shiny chrome of his car, and then into the distance the church spire tapering up into the sky until it seemed like a long needle. His knees had turned to water.

I am afraid of that man, that man Mr McSorley, Curly was saying to himself on the stepladder, stacking floor tiles on a shelf, when in walks Muldoon the crooked solicitor and tells him that the case is called for first Thursday in Michaelmas and to come in next day at his lunch break, so that they can get their act together. In his mind he now stood in the witness box, the judge firing questions at him, tripping him up, a barrister warning him that the case for the prosecution rested on his evidence. He saw himself being asked to stick out his tongue for the signs of a lie and he began to shake uncontrollably and the ladder underneath shook with him. He could do a runner, he could just vanish to some destinationless place, but where and how. He knew that he was being watched.

After work he went straight to Widow Nell's, not to the bar, but to the back room, where he sat at a table, by himself, lads saluting and gassing and he talking back but not knowing a single thing he said. There was a newspaper open on the table and a big article about the price of cattle feed gone sky high and fears for the decline in agriculture. The money in his granny's shed, his fingerprints on it. He should have used rubber gloves, but he didn't. He should have refused Donie, but he didn't. *I am so far in that I can't get out* was what he kept saying, kept piecing the bits together – if he denied what he saw that would be perjury and he would go to jail, and if he didn't deny that he saw what he saw the McSorleys would get him. Either ways he was sunk. When Curly was a young man, there was a girl two doors down that got a toy at Christmas that could talk. It was clothed in red fur, the mouth wide open and the tongue hanging out. It had two plastic knobs for eyes and an orange fur nose, and every so often it said 'Elmo wants you to know that Elmo loves you'. He was Elmo, only it was him saying it to himself – *I am so far in that I can't get out*. It wouldn't stop. Shelagh, the barmaid, an older woman, could see that he was upset and kept bringing him saucers of chips that were free and asking if he was sure he wanted another drink and oughtn't he be heading home for bed.

After he'd downed three pints, two large whiskies,

and a Bailey's liqueur, he felt better. All of a sudden he asked himself, 'Why should I stay here, why should I loiter?' and got up and went out, pulling up his hood.

He was not drunk but he was not sober as he got on his bicycle and pedalled and pedalled through the drizzly night. Up the high street, past the church, past the monument, and down the back road, where people jogged at all hours and were a menace. Up to the junction that forked to the main road with a sign that said 'Dublin', except that it was invisible, cars flying by at one hundred miles an hour. Then pedalling at breakneck speed to get to the far side, and three and a half miles along to the forestry gates. When he entered the forestry he felt safer, tarred avenue with trees on either side and the big lake still and black and glassy. Everything black, save for one little light in the turret window of the ruin of the Castle. He'd never noticed that light before, because he'd never set foot there at night. That little light belonged to his other life, before he fell into the clutches of the McSorleys and before he buried the cursed bag in his granny's shed.

When Curly didn't appear at the beep of the boss's hooter and when it was discovered that his bed wasn't slept in, it was expected that he would mooch into work at some point with a cock-and-bull story. But when he was not seen and not heard of for twenty-four hours and had not kept the appointment with Muldoon, the Gardai had to be alerted. A guard drove up to his granny's house and, being as she was an old woman, he didn't want to upset her too much, did not immediately get out his notebook and biro to take down any evidence. He was amazed at the amount of clobber she had accumulated, every single chair and armchair a throne of old newspapers and bags and flattened cardboard boxes. There were bits of crochet, dolls, dolls' prams, and a multitude of small china animals along the mantelpiece, above the unlit stove. Sensing that Curly was in some trouble, she got very flustered and jumped up and took her hat and coat off the hook on the hall stand saying 'What have I got to do now, sir,' and he had the greatest trouble in calming her down. He said to leave it to them, that Curly had not boarded bus or train, and that Gardai were following up every lead and had their ears close to the ground.

It was a German woman who found him, or rather traced the sound of a ringing telephone. Eerie it was, up there in that empty wilderness, her two big dogs chasing each other and sniffing the territory where they had never been before. She was new to the neighbourhood and had come to look at a portion of bog with a view to renting it, so that they could have a turf fire the year following. Various sections were pegged with names and numbers, but there were still allotments for rent.

The phone was almost buried in a thicket of golden-crown heather, the 'auroras of autumn', as she had read in the guidebook. The ringing stopped just as she got to it and, bending in the near dusk to pick the phone up, she was startled by the sight of a sneaker, a man's dirty white sneaker, at the side of a deep black trench. She backed away, not knowing which apparition would be more terrifying at that instant, that of one living or dead. The phone felt alive in her hand, like a viper, a pink viper, and she walked, or rather she ran, holding it and whistling sharply to call her dogs.

The guard who answered the intercom could not hear her very distinctly, but when he saw her walk into the station, he guessed by her expression that she had come with a story.

It was all over the town, how Curly was missing and how sad, how very sad. The divers were not expected until later, since they were dashing all over the country, but the superintendent was promised that they would come, even if it had to be at night. Rumours were rife and ominous. Those who had barely thrown a word to Curly were now picturing him, so harmless, going up the street in his old windcheater, his brown mop of wet hair over his wet rosy cheeks, recalling his little impertinences, going up to people in pubs and saying *Why can ye not talk to me* and crashing weddings because he loved, adored, the taste of champagne. Some said that it must have been a rotten footbridge that gave way under him and that most likely the bog hole he fell into was deep, or the woman would have seen him. One pundit said that he might not be found for hundreds of years like an Elkman. A more sinister theory was that he had been brought there in the black night by those who wished him gone and an extra twist to the various scenarios was that he had indeed been got rid of, but somewhere else, that the mobile phone and the shoe were a decoy and Curly was lost in the vast swells of the Atlantic Ocean.

Only Donie knew, or rather guessed, that Curly, having heard that he was to appear in court, lost the nerve and believed that the judge could read his mind and would trip him up, so that somehow he would have to own up to the stash in his granny's shed. That's why he went at night and salvaged the bag to bury it – it was for her. It was love of her. The minute the news broke, Donie drove to the grandmother's to give her some kind of comfort and felt a villain, an out and out villain. He saw how the carts in the shed had been overturned and the empty hole with dirty black slashed cobwebs. It was in the bog now, beyond the grasp of mankind. 'I wouldn't do any harm to you or to your granny,' he had told Curly and he meant it, but he did, he did do harm and he felt rotten. When Phonsie the car dealer asked him to hide the haul, he was promised a bonus and a scooter for Kathleen, so she could hop down to the shops or have her hair done, when she felt like it. He did it for graft.

Never before had there been a hearse parked on that isolated road that led to the bog. How grim and inhospitable the place was, not a single bird-note, a universe of black-brown, frozen over and luridly lit by the fitful flares of the torches. The divers brought the body up slowly and laid it on the bank for the sergeant to identify Curly. Then it was placed in the black zipper bag and carried ceremoniously on a stretcher of tarpaulin. It would be taken first to the morgue for forensic examination and then to the chapel where the mourners would foregather.

It was in an annexe between the bar and the kitchen, poorly lit, that Shelagh asked the sergeant if she could have a word with him. He had gone in very late for a pint, to try to wind down. He could feel the emotion in her, but he could not see her face very clearly. She wanted to know one thing. What did Curly look like when they brought him out. He thought before answering. He knew that she needed reassurance of some kind and he heard himself say, 'He was fairly close to perfect.' He saved her the other things, how Curly's clothes were all soggy, his face and hands ash white from being suspended in the freezing water, and that when they pulled him out, the diver had to wipe the frothy fluid around his mouth, the egg white stuff, before putting him in the body bag. He spared her that.

'And the cause of death?' she asked.

'Probably death by misadventure,' he said. Picking up the carving knife that was on a sideboard, she drew it in mock execution across her neck and said woefully, 'Poor Curly, a lamb to the slaughter.'

The tradition still held to lay down the sword for a funeral. Everyone came. Bouquets of flowers lined the entrance hall, Isolde's the most exquisite of all – blue and purple – not like any flowers that might grow in the ditches, but like flowers in a dream. Curly's granny had to be contained, kept from trying to open the sacristy door, believing Curly was in there, even though she had already seen him in the coffin and put one of her china mice in along with him. Donie stood at the back. He was over a barrel, hadn't slept. At moments he thought he was keeling over and had to grasp the baptismal font for balance. He saw the McSorley brothers in their long black coats of finest nap, pillars of neighborliness and loyalty, their wives weeping beneath their mantillas.

Father McDermott spoke fondly of Curly, his innocence, his always offering a helping hand, his love of shooting stars and his love of the small things in life, like being invited into a house for hospitality. He said how poignant that Curly should lose his young life in the very bog where, only the previous June, he had helped a neighbor to foot and stack turf and then, somewhat melodramatically, he said, 'Whom the Gods love die young.' Gazing out at his parishioners, he asked them not only to grieve for a sensitive youth of one score years, but to open their hearts and examine their consciences, and then he reddened and his voice grew vehement. Greed, he said, was ruining the country, people no longer showed the compassion that they once had, and while he was not pointing a finger at any single individual, he said someone must have known that Curly was in some sort of jinx to go riding off into a bog in the dead of night.

Then Curly's voice, sweet and boyish, filled the chapel as a tape of his party piece was played and the mourners wept openly –

> The walking man I am
> I've been down on the ground
> I swear to God
> If ever I see the sun
> For any length of time
> I can hold it in my mind
> I'll never again go underground

They were filing out now and Donie filed out with them. He would drive straight away to Phonsie's place. Phonsie was an affable man but a ruthless man and with a cock-up of this magnitude, anything could happen. He might be next, dispatched to the wild blue yonder. Being a third cousin, people shook his hand and offered their condolences, but he was miles away.

The strength in their hands was mighty.

Green Georgette

Thursday

Mama and I have been invited to the Coughlans. It is to be Sunday evening at seven o'clock. I imagine us setting out in good time, even though it is a short walk to the village where they live and Mama calling out to me to lift my shoes so that the high wet grass won't stain the white patent. I expect that Rita, the maid, will admit us and we will be ushered in to the room where the piano is. It is a black piano. I saw it the day the Coughlans moved here, saw four men drag it in, sweating and swearing, and when it was put down it emitted a little sound of its own, a ghostly broken tune.

They have been here almost four months. Mr Coughlan works in the bank and though they have a car, he walks to work each morning, setting out punctually at twenty minutes to nine and carrying a lizard-skin attaché case. He probably walks for the exercise, as he is somewhat podgy, and there are always beads of perspiration on his forehead. He is slightly bald. Adjacent to the bank is the River Graney, and faithfully he leans over the stone bridge to look down at the brown, porter-coloured water, or perhaps at the little fish, perches and minnows, that are carried along in the swift current. He ignores most people, giving a mere nod to one or two notables. He is not popular. His wife, on the other hand, is the cynosure of all. She is like a queen. There is not one woman who is not intrigued by her finery, her proud carriage, and her glacial smile. Every Sunday when she comes in to mass, people gawp and nudge, as she goes up the aisle to sit as near as possible to the altar. She has a variety of smart fitted costumes and oodles of accessories and brooches. When they first came it was February and she wore a teddy bear coat that had brown leather buttons with cracks in them. They looked like fallen horse chestnuts. Soon after that, she wore a brown bouclé coat that came almost to her ankles and she wore it open so as to reveal a contrasting coloured dress in muted orange. She has a butterfly brooch, an amber brooch with a likeness of a beetle, a long-leafed marcasite brooch, and a turquoise wreathed with little seed pearls. Her first name is Drew. Her sister Effie lives with them and she is far plainer, with only two outfits, both tweed. She wore a fox collar some Sundays, and the glassy eyes of the fox staring out looked quite sinister. She was in a convent, but left before taking her final vows and for reasons that remain muddied. She prays very steadfastly, eyes shut tight, and she keeps kissing her metal crucifix. Drew on the other hand looks straight ahead at the altar, as if she is perceiving some mystery in it. I try to manoeuvre a seat in front of her, so that I can turn round and stare at her, and take note of her little habits and how often she swallows. She blinks with such languor.

Mama says that we will have a scone before setting
out, as we are not certain if we are invited for eats. We
might go in by the side entrance, where there is a damp
path under a canopy of tarpaulin and a lawn roller that
is never moved. It depends if there is somebody already
looking from behind the window. My father has not
been invited, so it seems that it is an occasion for ladies
only. It will probably be Drew, Effie, Mama and me.
The little daughters are away at boarding school. They
are twins, Colette and Cissy, and I am glad that they are
absent, as I might be put in a separate room with them,
banished from the company of the grown-ups. I will not
say a word. I will not need to.

Our being invited is a miracle and came about in an
accidental way. The Coughlans were having a supper
party. The whole parish knew about it. They were having prawn cocktail to start, then suckling pig with apple
sauce, followed by chocolate éclairs and cream. Rita
boasted of it in the butchers, the hardware, and the three
grocery shops. The guests were other banking people
from far afield and a hunting lady separated from her
husband and known as a bit of a card. Yet on the day
of their supper party, calamity struck. The cream in the
creamery had turned sour. It seems the vats had not been
scalded properly and all the contents had to be thrown
out. Rita went to the various shops and all she could get
was one tin of cream, with a picture of a red carnation on
the label. Mrs Coughlan was livid. She said one does not

give tinned cream to people of note and that fresh cream must be found. Rita thought of us. She knew us well and used to come the odd Saturday to help my mother, but once she went to them she did not want to know us and looked the other way if ever we met. Nevertheless, she arrived with a jug and a half a crown in her hand and Mama said coldly, 'Hello stranger.' Rita said that they were in a terrible pickle, not being able to get fresh cream, and might Mama, in the goodness of her heart, help out. Mama did not say yes at once. She took Rita to task for being a turncoat and for not telling us that she would no longer come of a Saturday to scrub. Rita was very flustered, said she knew she had done wrong, that she was awake nights over it and was biting her nails. She showed her nails, which were certainly bitten down to the quick. Mama then got the white jug. It was a lovely long slender jug, with a picture of a couple in sepia, standing, modestly, side by side. There were three large pans of cream put to settle in the dairy and with the tips of her fingers, Mama skimmed the cream into the jug. She did it perfectly, making sure that no milk got in. The separated milk was a bluish white in colour, not like the butter yellow colour of the cream. She refused the money. Having been tart with Rita, she had now melted and gave her a bag of cooking apples in case they were short.

We heard that the party went off wonderfully. There were four cars with different registrations parked in the street outside and a sing-song after dinner. One lady guest could be heard in the public house across the road singing, 'There's a bridle hanging on the wall and a saddle in a lonely stall', screeching it, as the men in the pub attested to.

Mama says I am to wear my green knitted dress with the scalloped angora edging and carry my cardigan in case it gets chilly on the way home. It is about a half a mile's walk. She herself is going to wear her tweedex suit – a fawn, flecked with pink, one that she knitted for an entire winter. I know in her heart that she hopes the conversation will get around to the fact of her knitting it. Indeed, if it is admired, she will probably offer to knit one for Mrs Coughlan. She is like that. Certainly she will make Drew a gift of a wallet, or a rug, as she goes to the new technical school at night to master these skills. Nothing would please her more than that they would become friends, the Coughlans coming to us and a big spread of cakes and buns and sausage rolls and caramel custards in their own individual ramekins. She says that we are not to mention anything about our lives, the geese that got stolen up by the river at Christmas time, my father's tantrums, or above all, his drinking sprees, which blessedly have tapered off a bit. My father will insist that his supper be prepared before we leave and a kettle kept simmering on the stove, so that he can make a pot of tea. We will have put the hens and chickens in their hatches and, being still bright, we are bound to have trouble in coaxing them in. Quite soon after we arrive, it will be evident

whether or not there are to be refreshments. There will
be a smell from the kitchen, or Rita bustling, or Effie
going in and out to oversee things.

Monday

We went. Effie greeted us and saw us into the drawing
room, where Mrs Coughlan sat upright on a two-seater
sofa with gilt-edged side arms. She wore green georgette
and a long matching scarf which swathed her neck and
part of her chin. The picture instantly brought to mind
was one I had seen in a book at school, featuring an English lady, swathed in white robes and crossing the desert.
She let out a light, brittle laugh and her hand, when
it took mine, was weightless as a feather. 'Such pretty
ringlets,' she said, and laughed again. I was hearing her
voice for the very first time, and it was like sound coming
from a music box, sweet and tinkling. Turning to Mama,
she said how much she had been looking forward to the
visit and how terribly kind it was to give her that delicious cream. Instantly, they had a topic. They discussed
whether cream should be whipped with a fork or with
a beater, and they agreed that a beater in the hands of a
mopey girl, no names mentioned, could lead to having a
small bowl of puddiny butter.

There was a fire in the room, with an embroidered
screen placed in front of it. The various lit lamps had
shades of wine red, with masses of a darker wine fring-

ing. It was like a room in a story, what with the fire, the fire screen, the fenders and fire irons gleaming, and the picture above the black marble mantelpiece of a knight on horseback breaching a storm. I sat on a low leather pouffe, looking at Drew and then looking out the window at the setting sun, from which thin spokes of golden light irradiated down, then back on her, whose perfume permeated the room, and despite her bemused smile and the different and affecting swivel of hand and wrist, her eyes looked quite sad. I could not understand why she was swathed in that scarf, unless it was for glamour, as the room was quite warm. Effie was extremely nervy – she would begin a sentence but not finish it and from time to time slap herself smartly and mutter, much to the irritation of her sister. It struck me then that she probably had to leave the convent on account of her nerves. Moreover, she seemed on the verge of tears, even though she was telling us how well they had settled in, how they loved the canal and the boating, loved their walks in the wood road, and had made friends with a few people.

'Hugh doesn't love it,' Mrs Coughlan said, adding that he was too much of a loner. This gave Mama another opening in the conversation, admitting that after she had come back from America – something she was most anxious to be let known – she, too, had felt herself to be an outsider. Mrs Coughlan exclaimed and said, 'But why ever did you come home?' Mama explained that she had merely come on a holiday, and had got engaged, and soon after got married. A little sigh escaped them both. Mrs Coughlan said that Hugh would not be joining us, since he was painfully shy and a bad mixer. I expect he was in his own den doing figures, or maybe reading. She then uncrossed her legs and lifted the folds of green georgette a fraction, so that to my heart's content I was able to see her beautiful shoes. They were cloth shoes of a silver fili-gree, with purple thread running through the silver, and there was a glittery buckle on the instep. I could have knelt at them. Effie then excused herself, looking more teary than ever. Mama welcomed that, because I felt that she wanted to get confidential with Mrs Coughlan and to share views about marriage, childbearing, and the change of life.

'It's not a bed of roses, by any means,' Mama stark-ly announced, and Mrs Coughlan concurred. She even became a little indiscreet, said that on her wedding day three unfortunate things happened – the edge of her veiling got caught on the church railing as they posed for the photographs, the handle of the knife broke in the wedding cake as she cut it, and an old aunt swore that she saw a fat mouse move across the dining room of the hotel floor and went into hysterics. Then, casually, she mentioned that she had been married off in her twenties. I reckoned that she was about thirty-five or six. She said that small towns were stifling and that bank folk only talked shop. Moreover, every few years Hugh got trans-ferred to another town, so they could never put down roots and it was all ghastly. Mama sympathised, said she had once been in the same place for many years, but now loved her farm, her kitchen garden and her house, and would not be parted from them. Then she slipped in the fact that she hoped Mrs Coughlan would feel free to call on us, whenever she wished and this was met with tepid, absent-minded gratitude. Things were not going brilliantly. There was no ripple to it and there was no excitement. There were times when it seemed as if Mrs Coughlan had literally floated away from us, not listening, not seeing, lost in her own world-weary reverie.

A trolley was wheeled in. The china tea set was exquisite, with matching slop bowl, sugar bowl, and jug. The teapot was like a little kettle and had a cane handle. But the eats were not that thrilling. The sandwiches looked rough, obviously made by Rita, and I could swear that it was a shop cake. It had pink icing with a glacé cherry on top, not like Mama's cakes, which were dusted with caster sugar or a soft-boiled icing that literally melted on the tongue. There were also shop biscuits. Drew urged us to tuck in, as she refrained from food and kept feeling her throat through the layers of green folded georgette. Effie's hand trembled terribly as she passed us the cup and saucer, and Drew told her for goodness sake to get the nesting tables open so that we could at least have something to balance on.

Wanting desperately to show gratitude, Mama said that if ever they needed cream, fresh eggs, cabbage, or cooking apples they had only to ask. Normally she was reserved but her yearning to form a friendship had made her over-accommodating.

All of a sudden Drew got up and rushed to look in the oval mirror that had two candlesticks affixed to it, the white candles unlit, and unwinding the georgette scarf she sighed, saying to Effie to come and look, that the rash was much worse. Effie rushed to her, felt her glands, and said yes, that her lip had also swollen up. To our eyes there was no swelling at all, just a slightly chapped lip and a cold sore. Effie said they would ring the doctor at once, but Mrs Coughlan tut-tutted, said that was too much of an imposition and that they would go there instead. My heart sank. Mama's must have sank, too. Mama agreed with Effie that they should send for him and that he would come and bring several medicines in his doctor's bag. Drew was adamant and told Effie to run and get her fur coatee. She kept touching her lip and her glands with her forefinger, and Mama wondered aloud if perhaps it was some allergy, that maybe she had been gardening and touched nettles or some other plant, to which there came the distinct and crisp answer of 'Nouh'. Mama could not find the right thing to say.

Effie was back, all solicitude, putting the coatee around her sister's shoulders as they went out. We stood in the hall door to see them off, and Effie, who had only recently learned to drive, set out at a reckless speed. She could have killed someone. We debated as to what we should do, but the truth was we did not want to go home so early. Mama looked down at the perforated rubber mat that allowed for muck and wet to fall through and vowed that when she had a bit of money she would invest in one, so as not to be down on her knees scrubbing the kitchen floor and hall three times a week. It was not yet dark. Men were sitting on a bench across the road, drinking and talking quietly among themselves. They recognised us but did not call across, as by being in the Coughlan house we had somehow placed ourselves above them. Mama said that yes, the sitting room was nice, but it did not have a very salubrious view. It was a hushed night and there was a smell of flowers, especially night-scented stock from Mrs McBride's garden next door. Mrs McBride was a fanatic gardener and was forever wheeling different pots with flowering plants onto her front porch. We had heard that there was a rift between her and the Coughlans, as both had allotments at the back of their houses and there was argument about the boundary fence – so much so that a guard had had to be called to keep the peace.

We went back into the room and surprised Mr Coughlan, who was wolfing the sandwiches. The moment he saw us he made some apologetic murmur and bolted. Mama whispered to me that there was a strong smell of drink off him and said that no one ever knew the skeletons that lurked in other people's cupboards. She removed the fire screen and out of habit poked the fire and put a sod on it, and then she vetted the contents of the room more carefully, estimated the cost of all the furnishings, and said if she could have one item it would be the tea trolley and perhaps the mirror with the little candelabras on either side, but that she would not give tuppence for the piano. Then, as if I were absent, she said aloud to herself that there was no swelling and no rash, and that for a woman to wish to go to the doctor at that hour of evening was fishy, decidedly fishy.

'I adored her silver shoes,' I said, trying to sound grown up.

'Did you darling,' she said, but she was too busy cogitating matters such as how much did he drink, did husband and wife get on, and why were very young children in a boarding school, and why did the sister, the ex-nun, live with them.

The doctor was something of a ladies' man, and though Mama did not refer to it, it was known that he kissed young nurses in the grounds of the hospital and had taken a student nurse once to Limerick to the pictures, where they stayed canoodling for the second showing, much to the annoyance of the usherette. She conceded that though the green georgette dress and the shoes were the height of fashion, it was not the kind of attire to wear when going to a doctor. At that very moment and like a lunatic, I imagined Drew lying on the doctor's couch, he leaning in over her, patting her lip, perhaps with iodine, she flinching, her complexion so soft, a little flushed, and how both, as in a drama, had a sudden urge to kiss each other, but did not dare to. We sat for a bit and helped ourselves to some biscuits.

When they got back they showed real surprise at our being still there. I even think that Drew was irked.

'Nothing serious I hope,' Mama said, and Effie flinched and said that Drew had been given an ointment and also a tonic, because she was very run down. He had, it seems, checked her eyelids for anaemia. Drew looked different, as if something thrilling had happened to her, and was gloating over the fact that the doctor and his wife were on first names with her, as if they'd all known one another for an age. It seems they had to wait in the hall as the doctor was tending to an epileptic child, and while they were waiting, his wife came through and chatted with them, offered them a sherry and insisted that they call her Madeleine. Mama's hopes were thus dashed. The doctor's wife used to know us, used to visit us, which was such an honour and meant that we were people of note. Mama did things for her, like sew and knit and bake, and always kept a baby gin in a hidden drawer so that she could be given a tipple, unbeknownst to my father, when she came. Then she stopped coming, and much to Mama's bewilderment – we were never given a reason, and there had been no coolness and no argument. Months later, we heard that she told the draper's wife that our milk had a terrible smell and that she would not be visiting again. It had so happened that on one occasion when she came, the grass was very rich and hence the milk did smell somewhat strong, but being a town person she would not know the reason.

Effie then said that Drew should go straight to bed, and Mama concurred and asked if we might be excused. She was too conciliatory, even though she was rattled within.

'So glad you could both come,' Mrs Coughlan said, but it lacked warmth – it was like telling us that we were dull and lustreless and that we were not people of note.

'Well now I can say I met the grand Mrs Coughlan,' Mama said tartly as we walked home, and she repeated her old adage about old friends and new friends – when you make new friends, forget not the old, for the new ones are silver, but the old ones are gold.

We were in a gloom. The grass was heavy with dew, cattle lying down, munching and wheezing. She did not warn me to lift my feet in order to preserve my white shoes, as she was much preoccupied. There was no light from the kitchen window, which signified that my father had gone up to bed and that we would have to bring him a cup of tea and humour him, as otherwise he would be testy on the morrow.

I had this insatiable longing for tinned peaches, but Mama said it would be an extravagance to open a tin at that hour, while promising that we would have them some Sunday with an orange soufflé, which she had just mastered the recipe for. Mixed in with my longing was a mounting rage. Our lives seemed so drab, so uneventful. I prayed for drastic things to occur – for the bullocks to rise up and mutiny, then gore one another, for my father to die in his sleep, for our school to catch fire, and for Mr Coughlan to take a pistol and shoot his wife, before shooting himself.

Manhattan Medley

Midsummer night or thereabouts. The heat belching up from the grids in the pavement, trumpet, or was it trombone, and the hands of the homeless, the fingers thin and suppliant, like twigs, outstretched for alms. We were relative strangers to each other and strangers in that lively, pulsing city.

To leave a party that was held in your honour, we risked the odium of the ever-wrathful Penelope, but yet we did. You gave me the signal, a knowing glance and a nod, even as a coven of women had swarmed around you in evident and gushing admiration. Your scarlet cummerbund was much remarked upon.

On the stairway we accidentally kicked some marbled boules balls that were there as ornament and that came skeetering down along with us. Nor was that our only miscreance. In the pocket of your dinner jacket was a coffee cup, severed from its fragile handle, which had somehow affixed itself to my little finger. In order to avert a crisis, you simply put both in your pocket and mum was the word. It was a turquoise coloured cup and white handle with gold edging, which with a nicety you placed courteously by the foot scraper at the top of the flight of steep steps.

Cities, in many ways, are the best repositories for a love affair. You are in a forest or a cornfield, you are walking by the seashore, footprint after footprint of trodden sand, and somehow the kiss or the spoken covenant gets lost in the vastness and indifference of nature. In a city there are places to remind us of what has been. There is the stone bench for instance, where we sat that night to quench our thirst, but really to call into existence a wall with two water nozzles cemented together, metal tubers bearing the trade name 'Siamese'. A bit of concrete wall against which you threw me cruciform-wise to press your ebullient suit.

'Is there a place for me in some part of your life?' was what you asked. Yes. Yes, was the answer. We walked uptown and down, not knowing what to do with ourselves, not knowing whether to part, or to prolong the vertigo and sweet suspense. I asked what you thought of the tall, brown building that seemed to tilt like a lake above us, a brown lake of offices, deserted at that hour and poised as if to come heaving down into the street. You admired it but said you would have varied the cladding. I found the word so quaint and teased you over it. By asking for a place in the margin of my life, you were by inference letting me know that you also were not free, that you were married, something I would have assumed anyhow.

Only fools think that men and women love differently. Fools and pedagogues. I tell you, the love of men for women is just as heartbreaking, just as muddled, just as bewildering, and in the end just as unfinished. Men have talked to me of their infidelities. A man I met at a conference described to me how he had been unfaithful for twenty-odd years, yet upon learning of his wife's first infidelity, went berserk, took a car ride, beat up his opponent, came home, broke down, and sat up with her all night thrashing out the million moments and non-moments of their marriage, the expectations, the small treacheries, the large ones, and the gifts that they gave or had failed to give. Then, weary and somewhat purged, they had made love at dawn and she had said to him – this unslept, no-longer-young, but marvellous wife – If you must have an affair, do, but try not to, and he swore that he would not, but feared that somewhere along the way he would succumb, yield to the smarms of the Sirens.

Of all the things that can be said about love, the strangest is when it strikes. For instance, I saw you once in a theatre lobby in London and you struck me as a rather conventional man. I thought, there is a man with a wife and undoubtedly two motor cars, a cottage in the country to which he repairs at weekends, one car stacked with commodities, wine, cheeses, virgin olive oil, things like that, a man not disposed to dalliances. Maybe like my friend you have sat up with a wife one entire night, atoning, and maybe it seemed as if everything was forgiven, but something always remains and festers.

Of course, I knew you by reputation and read complimentary articles about your buildings, those wings and temples and rotundas that have made you famous and bear the granite solemnity that is your trademark. Between that austerity and your wine-red cheek, where the blood flowed in a velvety excitement at the dinner party, I saw your two natures at odds, your caution and your appetite.

We walked and walked. The truffle hound and his Moll, chambering. Then we stood outside my hotel and looked at the display in a glass case of the larger bedrooms, which were decorated in gold and apricot shades, with bright chintz upholstery. You did not come up. But it was a near thing, holding each other, unable to let go, and melting.

Your gift arrived the next afternoon, after you had left to go home to England. It was an orchid that stood in a cake box, the pot filled with pebbles, grey-white pebbles that recall wintry seashores. The white-faced petals high on the thin slender stalk, suggested butterflies poised for flight. Flight. Have you fled from me? I imagine not. Unable to sleep at night, I look at it, and from the slice of light that enters where the curtains do not meet, it looks somehow spectral.

You had put me in such a flowing state of mind and body that I determined to befriend all those whom I met. A tall black wraith of a man with one missing eye put his hand out imploring and I gave, liberally. He launched into an irrational spiel of how he had fought in the Civil War, to defend the right of God and man, had been there alongside Ulysses S. Grant. The fawn flap over the missing eye was pitiful. He walked along with me, unwilling to cut short his lament.

Strange how suited we were. The right height, the right gravity, the right tongues and oh, idiocy of idiocies, the right wall. Does something of us remain there, some trace, like the frescoes in caves, scarcely visible? You asked if we might make love in all the capital cities throughout the world, if we might go to them in secrecy and return in secrecy, hoarding the sweet memories of them. We would not enter into a marriage that must by necessity become a little stale, a little routined. Yes, yes was the answer. Yet the friend Paul who saw us leave Penelope's gathering said that I looked back at him disconcerted, like Lot's wife before she was turned into a pillar of salt.

An affair. It is a loaded word. A state of flux, fluxion. So many dire things happen, plus so many transporting things. Letters get opened by the wrong source or the gift of a trinket gets sent to the wrong address by a novice in the jewellers. A woman I know secretly read the list that her husband's newest mistress had jotted down for her Christmas stocking – Krug champagne, lingerie, a bracelet, and last, but by no means least, a baby. Yes, in capitals – A BABY. The wife went into action. She took him to the Far East on a cruise, to various islands, all very rustic, remote, wooden boats with wooden chairs, huts to sleep in, dancing girls and garlands of gardenias put around the necks of this mistrustful pair. Before they left home, the wife had done something rather clever and rather vicious. She had sent the predatory young woman copies of other letters written by other women, enabling her to see the graspingness and the similarity of these missives, reminding her that unfortunately she was one of many. A touch of the Strindberg. Another woman told me that she first got a whiff of her husband's affair, not from rifling his pockets, but from the simple fact that when his mistress came to their house for cocktails, she brought her rival a bunch of dead flowers. Carnations. Later that evening, when they had all repaired to a restaurant, she saw husband and mistress in cahoots, then remembered the dead flowers, stood up and made her first ever, somewhat pathetic scene – 'I am going to the bathroom now and then I am going home', was what she had said. He did not follow immediately, but soon after he did and found her on a sofa eating the flowers as if they were coconut shreds, then spitting them out, and he simply said that he hated scenes, women's scenes, then went out onto the balcony and walked up and down, but stayed, as she said, stayed.

Clarissa calls me from the west coast most days. I met her after I had given a lecture out there and she sensed that we had something in common. A little thing happened to unite us. The contents of her bucket handbag fell out and I said, 'What's wrong Clarissa, what's wrong,' at which she turned and asked if I believed she was having a breakdown. She is seeing a trauma specialist. Her mother, whom she scarcely knew, has recently died and in the wake of this death, a mountain of troubles has assailed her. Her mother's death has opened a trap door into the unknown. Her mother, who was beautiful and also rich, never really discussed things, and this now is causing Clarissa to drop handbags, over-salt the food, and have a sherry in the morning, she who does not even like drink. She wants to ask her dead mother a key question about a naked man in her bedroom. She was a toddler who had ambled across a landing, whereupon the mother shouted at her to get out. The man must have been an old flame. At camp, to which she was sent aged twelve, she saw a photograph of a woman who resembled her mother and kissed it when others were out of sight. She kissed it, and at home she smelt a nightgown that was hanging forlornly in a wardrobe. It smelt of mother. She has something important to tell me but she does not know how to say it. She trusts me because of the debacle of the handbag.

Graffiti, graffiti, graffiti. They seem to be done by the same unseen hating hand. Parables of rage. On walls, on vans, even on the torn leatherette of the back seat of a taxi. The driver was angry. His photo staring out of a hanging tag showed a disappointed, no longer young man. Suddenly he was shouting to another driver who cut in on us. Then he railed against the jarvey cars, horses fouling the street, pissing artificial flowers clipped to the side of their carriages.

When they drank a toast to you at Penelope's dinner party, I could see that you were nervous, your face flushed from the blaze of candle flame. We were not at the same table, but in the same archipelago, as you said. You were talking to a woman, and I knew by your hesitance that you knew she desired you and that you could not return her ardour. She spilt red wine on her thigh and pleaded for sundry advice. Someone suggested white wine to neutralise the red; someone else suggested salt and handed you a dainty silver cruet, with which to minister to her. It was then you looked across at me; it was then you caught my eye through the spaces between the trellises of branching candelabra. You gazed, indifferent to the red and white wine that flowed in an estuary on the woman's thighs. In that milieu of high society, scorching flame, and brittleness, we fell. Later, when we had all stood up to repair to the salon for coffee, you saw me link a man, both to be friendly and marginally to nettle you. Quite testily you nudged me, 'Am I taking you home or have you better fish to fry?'

I wish you were only torso, only cock. No pensive eyes to welcome me in or send me packing. No mind to conjure up those qualms that clandestine lovers are prone to. No holdall of incumbents – mother, father, wife, child, children, all, all calling you back, calling you home. I wish

I were only torso in order to meet you unencumbered. I recall an image on a postcard from the seventh century, that of a headless woman, a queen, leaning a fraction to one side, her robe torn, breasts like persimmons, one arm missing, yet pregnant with her own musks.

I have been to our wall, to pay my respects. You would think it was the Wailing Wall in Jerusalem, where I once was and stuck a petition written on a piece of paper, in between the cracks. People see me standing by our shrine but make nothing of it, for they are just loitering. It is a city of nomads. You see a man or a woman with carrier bags or without carrier bags, walk up to a corner, cogitate and walk back in the direction from which they came. Everyone eats on the street, discarded hollows of bread, stumps of pickled cucumber, noodles phosphorescent in the sunlight, fodder for the starving. People sit on steps or sit at empty outdoor tables and stare. The place is teeming with the lonely and the homeless, both. One such woman, who sits by a fountain for hours each day, was, or so I was told by another woman, a bridesmaid at Grace Kelly's wedding, but came down in the world and went cuckoo. Cuckoo is a word they use a lot. Why is the cuckoo always a she? Treachery perhaps. Woman's treachery, different to man's. A mutual woman friend said your name, said it several times in my hearing, to unnerve me. Her eyes glittered like paste jewellery, that pale unchanging glitter, which palls. The canker of jealousy, jealousies. 'I don't want to see you get hurt', your best buddy Paul said, having observed us slip away from the party. Waspishly, he then mentioned how slender your wife was.

A tall red-bearded figure, a 'Finn McCumhal' of the pavement, with green eyes, is enfolded in a tartan rug, which he wears toga-wise. He sells things – cheap abstract prints, black and white cubes, and the wounded orchids of Georgia O'Keefe that appear both spent and fertile. I give him a coffee in the mornings, since he is stationed outside the deli. I asked him if he ever felt down in the dumps. He looked surprised. Said never. He was a mountain man and a Green Beret man. 'Plus, I have God.' Yes, that was his reply – 'Plus, I have God.'

Hot food.

Home-made pizza.

Warm brisket.

I could scarcely eat. I had gone downtown to do some chanting, to chant the taste, the smell, the touch, the after-touch and the permeability of you out of my mind. I thought I knew the building from a previous excursion, but found myself in wrong hallways, talking to janitors, who were surprisingly friendly, the old homeland and so forth. I went back into the street to telephone information. The kiosk looked to have been someone's abode – a dirty baseball cap, punched cans, orange rinds and a cassette tape in such a tangle that it looked as if it might presently scream. On the wall there was a card with neat lettering – 'WordPerfect in ten hours: Lotus.' WordPerfect in what? Further up the street were two pugilistic women, denouncing pornography. They held up photographs of sliced breasts hanging off, their voices rasping above the roar of traffic and sirens.

In a café, a newly married woman at a table next to me gave a dissertation to her friend on marriage, 'Yes . . . it's good to be married . . . he's a great anchor, Frank . . . I wouldn't have said that six months ago, but I do now . . . not overnight do you trust a husband, but it comes . . . it comes.' Then she dilated on their getting a dog. Her husband wanted a large dog, a Labrador. She wanted no dog. Eventually they settled on a small pedigree poodle as being a compromise between no dog at all and a large dog. They have named her Gloria, after Gloria Swanson.

Clarissa called very early. There was something she needed to tell me. She has had female lovers as well as male. It is not that she is promiscuous, her needs change. I asked her what it was like. She said it was a hunger for a ghost, a hunger not altered by man or woman and not altered by marriage. Then she said something poignant. She said the reason that love is so painful is that it always amounts to two people wanting more than two people can give.

My room is a rose pink with gilded mirrors and a chaste white bureau, which looks like a theatre prop. The centre drawer does not open, the side ones do. On the white lining paper of one, I wrote 'Remember.' I wrote it with the expensive pen you gave me, as we were parting, asking me to send you a word, words. Even though you hadn't come up that first night, I knew you wanted to, and I stood in my bedroom doorway, watching as the lift door was opened each time and people were disgorged, some boisterous, one couple gallingly amorous, and others weary from the day's hassle.

One young creature yesterday, on her throne of rubbish, wept. It was in front of a very select jewellers. I asked why she was weeping so. A man had played a dirty trick on her. He had put a hundred dollar bill in her white plastic cup and then taken it back. There had been an altercation. In the window behind her, a ruby necklace blazed on a dainty velvet cushion and a note simply said, 'circa 1800', but no price. Yes, a man had played a dirty trick on her. The word dirty had set me thinking. Had there been a proposition of some kind? Further along, a man dangled his empty cap and urgently said the same thing, again and again – 'I'm broke I'm homeless I'm broke I'm homeless' – scratched his bald head, saying he had travelled hundreds of miles from Georgia. Across the street came a more vociferous voice, shouting, calling it a city of abuse, a shit-hole, a hell-hole and saying that everyone sucked. The cart, which he must have taken from a supermarket, was lined with magazine covers featuring the latest movie stars. On the wall above him, someone had written, 'You're dead'.

I have never felt so alive, so ravenously alive. I walk for miles and miles. Yesterday evening the sky darkened and thunder began to rumble as if marching in from the back woods, from Georgia itself, marching in on the city and on the elect in limousines, stately as hearses, impervious to the plight of wretchedness. I saw the fiend urinate on the roped muscles of the movie stars and laugh wildly. His cart was a swamp. Outside a restaurant a man was bent over a refuse bag. What struck me was his hair. A short bouclé crop of it, Titian-coloured. He had the stealth of a hunter. What he hauled out was a loin bone, with shreds of meat half cooked and dripping. Without ado he began to gnaw. His eyes were incomparably placid. I thought to approach him to give him some coins but did not dare. The pupils of his eyes were too proud and full of distance, that unfathomed distance of the deprived. Moreover, his orgy with the bone was utter.

Stella, a friend from long ago, invited me to a hen party at her sister's house. It was out of town. Down in the dark cavern of an underground I could not find a single human being who might direct me towards the right track. A mass of people in mindless urgency hurtling through the turnstiles and with no time to speak. I came up and hailed a taxi. Passing row after row of identical tall blocks of flats, and occasionally from a billboard sighting a glamorous face, male or female, peddling cosmetics or trainers or a television station, I had this impatience to get to Stella's house and leave presently, because I was convinced that you were returning to this city in search of me. I even imagined you sitting in an armchair in the undistinguished lobby, watching the swing doors for my return. Stella's sister's house was a white clapboard, identical houses all along the street, and mown lawns, and a sense of everything being neat and hunky dory. The women guests were of two kinds – those who were slightly shy, wore long skirts and sandals, and the go-getters in very short skirts and slashed hairdos, all blonde. 'What hat de clock,' one woman said, remarking on the fact that the root of the English language had originated in her part of Saxony. Her husband had but recently left her for a younger woman. Stella wore a stricken look. She stood in the dining room, her small child clinging to her, holding a handful of cutlery and trying by her expression to tell me that much had happened since we last met. 'In a moment, pet,' she kept saying to her second daughter, who had a silvered paper crown, which she needed to be clipped to her hair. Stella's sister Paula was an altogether more assertive type, and looking through the French windows into the garden, she complained about the table being unlaid.

'I ironed the cloth,' Stella said feebly. It was only half ironed. The creases on it were a mimicry of tiny waves upon water. It had begun to drizzle. The glasses in which the drinks were going to be served had incrustations of fruit. Pineapple and melon in ungainly wedges. Each woman arrived bearing a gift. It was a birthday for an elderly aunt, who was sitting in an armchair, dazed.

As she was handed a bunch of white roses, her eyes filled up with tears and she held them to her chest as if she was holding an infant. The woman who brought the roses wanted Bourbon and inveighed against iced tea, which was being passed around. Another, who had that morning arrived from Europe, said she had found the perfect cure for jet lag. Wherever you are, or happen to be, you simply alter the time on your clock and get on with things. She was of the thin brigade, the hem of the red skirt level with her crotch. 'What hat de clock.' I ground a biscuit out of irritation. Stella got down on her knees to pick up the crumbs and by mistake overturned a glass. She asked if I remembered Mrs Dalloway, how much we both loved Mrs Dalloway, who threw a shilling in the Serpentine, bought flowers in Bond Street, and wished that she could live her life all over again, live it differently, as we assumed. The rain by now was coming down in buckets and loneliness seeping into me. I thought I wanted to think only of you and to think of you I would have to be alone. Paula, who was making a raspberry salad dressing, said I could not leave so abruptly, but I did. I was given a present on the way out, and in the street I opened the red crepe wrapping. It was a ladle onto which the rain fell in fat spatters, and standing there in that leafy suburban limbo, I thought of you with every pore of my being, drew you into me as if you were sun, moon, and rain, praying that nothing would cancel those journeys to cities around the world.

I went to Penelope's townhouse near the river, where we had met. So many quickening memories. It looked ghostly, black-veined creeper over the brick wall and no sign of life within and no coffee cup by the foot scraper. In the little walkway, by the railings, were the invalids and their nurses. Nurses in starched uniforms standing rigid, behind the wheelchairs. It was the invalids that unsettled me most. The spleen in their expressions was quite shocking and quite pitiless. It was like a sick room there, although we were out of doors. Somehow, the sight of them recalled those sad, studious, forgotten misfits in some of Rembrandt's haunted interiors. Their eyes frightened me most. Eyes onto which pennies would soon be pressed. Their lives, their youth, even their wealth, was already dead to them, and I thought, I am alive, you are alive, and remembered in detail the night of our simmer, your throwing me against the wall in an urgency, as if you intended to smash my bones.

Mercedes cleans the room. She is from Colombia. We have got into the habit of chatting. Frequently she cries, her tears are torrents. Some months ago her man failed to come home, he who had shared her bed for over a year. Only next day at work did she learn why. He had had a massive heart attack while holding the car door open for his boss and had died in an ambulance on the way to the hospital. Neither the boss nor any of the people in the apartment building knew of the man's relationship with her, because of their not being married. It was discovered by a note in his pocket, on which was written her name and address. His funeral, which she had to arrange, was a bleak affair – only a lawyer, herself, and one wreath. Chrysanthemums she thinks, fattened with eucalyptus leaves. His wife, from Jamaica, is strenuously making her claims. First it was his satin waistcoat, then his watch, then his engraved cufflinks, and then the one valuable watercolour that he possessed. She dreads that his wife will come and occupy the apartment. She has had to bring her brother from Colombia to stay indoors all day and keep guard. He plays the guitar and eats incessantly. Every day she says the same prayer, asks God to help her to bear it, and embraces me as if I had some influence in that quarter. She says he was the kindest man that ever lived, washed her feet, pared her corns, indulged her. She also says that if I can get a photograph of you or a sample of your handwriting, she can have a friend do a voodoo spell. It involves the blood of cockerels, but she assures me that it is not sinister.

Clarissa has guessed my predicament. I am invited to the coast. She has a cottage for me in the grounds. We make no secret of our muddles. She says to have a woman carnally opens up as many minefields as to have a man. She thinks a visit might help me. She is not sure about you. She has misgivings. She thinks you might be a philanderer. I tell her that is not so. I bought an English newspaper, to somehow reach you. Reading one of the supplements, I began to picture little hamlets, steep country roads, the faded coats of arms on manor gates, old people's homes, and flutes of white convolvulus attaching themselves to everything within reach. Then the picture slid into night, that hushed, de-peopled time of night, when the cottages that Shakespeare occasionally wrote of, are sunk in dew, poplars like ghosts along a hillside, fairy lights still twinkling outside the shut public houses, and I thought of you as being part and parcel of that landscape and prayed that you would admit me to it, to those cold mocking sensibilities, to those men and women sprung from the loins of admirals. I wonder why you chose me. A death perhaps. Often it is the death of a close one that sends us in search, so that we run here, there and everywhere, run like hares, knowing that we cannot replace that which is gone.

I detest these cosy hush-hush affairs, which your kind excels at. Women in their upstairs drawing rooms, made up to the nines, at lunch hour, standing by the folds of their ruched curtains, with glazed smiles. Sherry and gulls' eggs in wait. The marital chamber stripped of all traces of a spouse. Lamb cutlets and frozen peas and lots of darling, darling.

When one is smitten, what does one want imparted and what hidden? If for instance you say 'I am hell to live with', it has a certain bravura to it. Does it simply mean that you are lazy and sullen indoors, expect someone else, a wife or a servant, to pour the coffee or to put a log on the fire, but that you show yourself to best advantage when visitors are heard coming up the path, just as you are decanting the choicest wine? How I hate these games and subterfuges. Sunday lunches, Sunday dinners, Sunday teas, the gibberish that gets trotted out. A woman telling the assembled guests how clever her Dave is, while notching up grievances inside. It's ubiquitous. I was with a couple one Sunday when the wife pronounced on some book of poetry, whereupon her husband said 'Have you read it', and oh the look, the withering look that she gave back to him, saying have *you* read it, and in the icy aftermath, the hatred congealed.

The most telling moment was when you saw me in that crowded nightclub come up from the Ladies, utterly lost. It was bedlam. You were leaving the next morning. I had to make my way back to our long table and took a detour so that I would have to pass closer to you, but of course not touch you. Suddenly you stood up and said my name with great anxiety, as if we were about to be separated. Then you kissed me. They saw you kiss me and were surprised by your indiscretion. I don't remember how I got to my chair.

Again and again I pay my respects to our wall. Last evening, I went on a little foray before dark. The violet hour was quite beautiful, balmy and pregnant with the kind of promise that evening in this city heralds. Musicians had gathered and taken up their posts at several corners. Skeins of sound sweetening the air. At one corner an African boy held up his wares, ropes of pearls and scarves that fluttered like veiling. They looked quite magic. The whites of his eyes were orbs, full of the wonder of evening, the wonder of Africa, the sense of a day almost done. It mattered not to him that I didn't buy anything, that I ignored his entreaties to look. The violet hour. The homeless had already decamped for the night, in doorways, in recesses, on church steps, lying there in heaps, like sacks of potatoes. I saw one sleeping man pat his stomach and smile benignly. Perhaps he was dreaming of food, not the oily noodles left as refuse, but a banquet such as he had glimpsed through the window of some restaurant, a bounteous offering, the fruits of the earth. To think that he would waken hungry. Hungers of every denomination are on display.

Thunder shook the foundations of the hotel, but I was shaking anyhow. I had wakened from a dream of having telephoned your hotel in Paris, thereby showing my need. I was told that you were out. I telephoned again and again. At one minute to midnight I called again, but was told that you had not returned. Then five minutes later, when I called back, I was put through and you answered gruffly, having gone to sleep. I reckoned that you must have come in tired, or maybe a little drunk, and flopped down on your bed. In the dream, you recognised my voice immediately and asked how I knew that you were in such and such a hotel in Paris. I put the phone down because I sensed the naked terror of a man who believes he has just been trapped. It freaked me.

Without any deliberation, I decided what I must do. I rang the airline and found they had spare seats, probably because it was midweek. I decided to take up Clarissa's invitation, to spring a surprise on her. The guest bungalow has its own kitchen and a little patio that opens onto a garden. I imagine at this time of year there will be those sharp, needly red flowers that resemble the beaks of tropical birds, and the pale pink corollas of flowering cacti, in terracotta pots. Why I imagine this, is beyond me.

No doubt the atmosphere at supper will be tense and there will be plenty of wine and false gaiety to relieve the strain, because strain there must be, considering the undercurrents. Clarissa is unsure, recognising that she has a reliable husband in Todd, but keeps harking back to a favourite story by D. H. Lawrence, in which a woman rides into the desert, where she is stripped not only of her clothing and her worldly possessions, but stripped of her former self and her attachments.

Clarissa comes each morning, laden with boxes of tiles and grout and phosphorescent paints. She arranges the shells in panels and fonts, magical configurations for houses and grottoes, bringing the whoosh of the ocean and intimations of the disgorged creatures that once lived and throve inside them.

Your name comes up all the time and the very utterance

of it sends shivers through me. I have shown her one or two of your postcards, the more elliptical ones, but not of course, your letters. She has her doubts. Even your handwriting she questions. She cites clandestine loves in life and literature strewn with concealment, jealousies and betrayals. But I tell her, it has already begun. Even if I lingered here, there or anywhere it would still run its course, in letters, in longings and the whet of absence.

Not to go to you is to precipitate the dark and yet I hesitate. It is not that I do not crave the light. Rather, it is the certainty of the eventual dark.

Send My Roots Rain

Men and women hurled themselves through the revolving door of the hotel with an urgency, and so quickly did they follow one upon the other that Miss Gilhooley imagined it was bound to end in a stampede. Discharged into the hotel lobby, they flung out their arms or tossed their scarves, triumphant at having arrived. Miss Gilhooley drew back, waiting, as she hoped, for a pause in the hectic proceedings. It was then that Pat-the-Porter noticed her, standing somewhat tentatively on the lower entrance step – not a young woman but a striking woman in a gray Cossack hat, such as he had seen on an actress in a Russian film many years before. He held the door and drew her in, as he put it, 'to the most distinguished address in Dublin'. He was an affable man, with sparkling blue eyes, proud of his girth inside that fine uniform and certain of the importance of his station. He had, as he soon told her, been working there for thirty-three-odd years, barring the two years when the establishment was closed for the massive revamp.

The hall was a veritable Mecca. Marble floors of shell pink, which an unthinking being could easily slide on, and countless chandeliers, blazed and gave out a beautiful light, that surpassed daylight and trembled within the many mirrors. A fire was blazing and on either side were dented leather buckets filled with consignments of logs and turf. The flower arrangements were particularly fetching – golden gladioli and lilies in high vases and then nests of littler vases, which had deep blue orchids that had been severed from their stems squeezed inside, their faces pressed close to the glass, chafing at their imprisonment.

Pat-the-Porter was regaling her with some of the hotel's history from the time when it had opened its doors in 1824 – the perilous days during the Rebellion of 1916, when gunfire whizzed in Stephen's Green across the road, and sure, wasn't the lounge famous for having been the very place where the Irish constitution was drafted. In between these snatches of history, he snarled at young boys, bellhops, with their grey pillbox hats set at jaunty angles, reminding them of their various charges and all smiles. The couple in the Horseshoe Bar, as Pat-the-Porter said, were still waiting for their oysters, and the front steps needed more salt; he didn't want people breaking their ankles or their hips or any part of their anatomy. He was able to change his manner at a wink, soft and confiding with her, severe with the underlings, and giving a knowing half nod to the various swanks and habitués who came skiving through the swing doors and headed for either of the two bars or the Saddle Room. He would give her a booklet later on in which she could read all about the hotel, from its inception to the present time as a hot-spot for movers and shakers, not to mention the English gentlemen who came for the stag parties.

Miss Gilhooley, he opined, would feel more at home in the sedate ambience of the Lord Mayor's Lounge, and so he escorted her to a table that was not too close to the entrance, in a recess, a little round table covered with a white linen cloth and on which there rested a folded menu. The elderly pianist, in an excess of energy, was bent over his piano, hitting the keys so fervently that a waltz sounded like a recruiting song. His bald pate glistened in the winter sun that poured through the bay window and onto his knitted grey-white eyebrows and his small purple dickie-bow.

It would be true to say that her heart fluttered somewhat. Strange to think that she was about to come face-to-face with a great poet whom she rated above all other poets and especially the young whippersnappers with their portfolios of clever words and hollow feelings. His poetry evoked the truth of the land, dock and turnips and nettles, men behind their ploughs, envying the great feats of Priam and Hector, tormented men in small fields battling their desires. Again and again she recommended his poems to borrowers in the library where she worked, and once, she organised a little entertainment, where there were readings of his poems and refreshments afterwards. The audience was restless, finding the poems too depressing, so that there was fidgeting and coughing throughout.

Each time a new poem of his appeared in a newspaper she cut it out, assembling a scrapbook of him. Finding one addressed to a woman, whose name he wrote, she thought, he is not made of stone after all. They had first communicated some years before when she asked if she could impose upon him to sign a copy of his collected poems, to be placed in a glass cabinet in the library hall. He sent a white, ruled, adhesive sheet, which carried his name and the date, February twenty-second. It was in deep black ink and the handwriting being so cramped and tiny she felt he had a reluctance in writing it or sending it at all. The photograph on the back cover showed a formidable man, his forehead high and domed, the eyes hidden behind thick horn-rimmed spectacles.

One autumn night, in an expansive mood, she sat down and wrote him a letter about the white mist. It appeared from time to time, wraith-like, twining the three adjacent counties: frail as lace and yet sturdy as it wandered, or rather seemed to float above the fields, above the numerous lakes and separating into skeins and then meshing again. He wrote back warning her not to get too carried away by the mist and concluded by saying, 'I reject miracle in every form and shape.'

Now, she was here, picturing him arriving, somewhat awkward, in a long overcoat, looking around and being looked at, because he was famous and rumoured to be fiercely abrupt with any who ventured near him. She had come for poetry and not love, as she kept reminding herself. Miss Gilhooley had had her quota of love, but had never managed to reach the mysterious certitudes of marriage. In her small town she was mockingly referred to as the Spinster.

She began imagining things they might talk about at first, the changes that had occurred in their country, changes that were not for the better, bulldozers everywhere and the craze for money. Money, money, money. The rich going to lunch in their helicopters, chopping the air and shredding the white mist, their wives outdoing each other with jewellery and finery, stirring their champagne with gold swizzle sticks, and Mrs Ambrose boasting about their drapes from the palazzo of a gentleman in Milan and a tea-set shipped from Virginia that had once belonged to a president of the United States. Pictures on their walls of bog and bogland, where they no longer set foot, priceless pictures of these lonesome and beautiful landscapes and pictures of bog lilies that lay like serrated stars on pools of purple-black bog water. It was not only the rich but those who aped them that were also money mad. That little hussy who sued the Church Fathers because the sleeve of her coat singed as she was lighting a candle, actually employed the family solicitor to press for compensation and he did, egging her on, encouraged her in this rotten ploy.

The invitation to meet had come some weeks after Christmas, but the stamps on the envelope had pictures of various snowed-on Santa Clauses, so it seemed that he had deliberately delayed posting it or else it had lain in his coat pocket.

Though frozen, when she arrived, one of her cheeks was now scalding from the blaze of the fire and the pile of ash under the grate that was a molten red. She moved her chair back a fraction, as she did not want to be flushed when he arrived. She reckoned on his being late, poets always were. Her bus journey had been long and cheerless, the fields along the way flecked with snow, and in places small mounds of snow lay like hedgehogs crouching inside their own igloos. She had walked briskly from the bus station through the busy streets, strains of music, melodeon and guitar, fraught young mothers wielding their pushchairs, and beggars of various nationalities. She stopped by one older woman because of the little begging bucket, a blue bucket such as a child would take to the seaside with his spade to make a sand castle, and soon regretted her mistake in trying to have a conversation, as the woman had a cleft palate and could scarcely pronounce her own name, which was Mary. A frost, sheer and unblemished, coated the bonnets of the cars that were like sentinels around the grand garden square, and the railings, clad with icy snow, felt damp through the palm of her glove. She stopped a second time to admire a statue of Wolfe Tone, flanked by tall columns of stone, the valorous figure sprung, as it were, from earth, the green-bronze of his boots, his jacket and his torso, curdled and glinting in the wintry sun.

Though feeling hot she felt too constrained to remove her coat, merely opened the top buttons and let it fall capewise over her shoulders as she gradually eased her arms out of the sleeves. Under no circumstances would she mention the fact that she had written snippets of her own locality, little nothings for which she had received a flurry of rejection slips, polite and useless. There was one literary editor who had befriended her and who believed that one day she might become a Poet and in his tutoring of her became a little smitten. He would take her for a drive each week, to discuss this or that piece of writing and always on the dashboard there was a packet of toffees or glacier mints for her to take home. Eventually, they drove a distance away to the seaside, whence they would get out of the car and look or listen as the Atlantic waves vented their fury and now and then surprise them with a rogue wave that sent them toppling. One evening at dusk, when she could not see his face, he said that he was happy with the woman to whom he had been married for many years, but that those drives, the two of them witness to the hungers of the sea and the cry of the seagulls, were dear to him. Though young, she sensed for the first time how inexplicable love was.

She had been in love more than once, gloriously, breathlessly in love, but it was the last attachment that had been the deepest, that was as she believed, ordained. Such happiness. The long walks at weekends, scaling mountains which she would never have done alone, but she felt safe and confident next to him, and indeed if she missed her footing, as she often did, he was there to catch her and plant a kiss. Once they were loaned a grand house in County Galway and in the evening went to the pub in the hotel and talked with the beaters and the gillies and it was there she learned the yodel used to raise woodcock – 'Waayupwaayupwaayup'. It became their favorite password. By the open fire she read poetry to him, read from a book of foreign poets with the English translation on the opposite page and they swore that they would learn languages, that she would learn French and he Spanish and would converse in their adopted tongue. In one letter she was rash enough to tell him that she would walk water to reach him and he replied in kind. It was reciprocal.

His letter breaking it off was wedged half in and half out of her letterbox. She thought that he was merely postponing a date they had made to meet in Dublin at the end of the month, but she was wrong. He praised her qualities in English and in Irish and she cursed him for not having had the gumption to tell her in person. She hid it so as to return it to him in due course, but put it somewhere so safely that she could not remember where that safe place was.

'They'll find it, when I'm dead,' she said spitefully.

After the initial shock she felt the magnitude of the loss, and her whole will was directed towards getting him back. She so convinced herself of this that she bought wooden tubs to plant bulbs in the garden and new towels that were stacked in the bathroom, on a stool, waiting for him. They were a beautiful oatmeal color. She lost friends, having no time for them and they, for their part, were aghast at how she was letting herself go, hair wild and uncombed, her clothes streelish, she who had once been so proud of her appearance. Her boss in the library – a sombrous man – asked if she had had a bereavement, to which she could only reply, yes, yes. After work she went straight home and locked her door and before sleep she would wait for his footsteps, thought she heard a friendly tapping on the windowpane. How often did she switch on the light, stare into the empty room and curse her daft imaginings. She turned to poets as she would to God. Gerard Manley Hopkins was her favourite poet at that time and the line she repeated again and again and which incurred much disparagement, was 'O thou Lord of life, send my roots rain.'

Hearing of a psychic in another country, who lived on a caravan site, she drove there one Saturday and begged, yes begged, for a reading. How her spirits lifted when the woman described in detail things that had actually happened, a hand-painted scarf which her lover had given her and which he placed shyly on her head in the shop, and the time that they had met by surprise in a hotel, their astonishment as they withdrew to an alcove and without exchanging a word, his placing his hand on her chest to calm the violent heartbeats. The psychic then foresaw them setting up house together. It was a cottage by the sea, which they would do up and extend. She drew a picture of their future life together, one or other, whoever got back first of an evening, kneeling to light a fire and praying that the chimney would not smoke, though at first it would, but in time that would clear, once the flue had its generous lining of soot. So real did this become for Miss Gilhooley that she began to furnish the imaginary house, choose wallpapers for various bedrooms, bathroom tiles with specks of gold, such as she had seen in a catalogue and she also added a balcony to the main bedroom where they would stand at night and hear the roaring waves and in the sunny mornings watch the several waterbirds wade gracefully on the soft muddy shore.

Her only sensible action during that wretched time was not to take the pills the doctor insisted she must take. One evening at dusk she drove to the lake, unscrewed the can and dropped the contents into the dark water that was scummed with debris. Many secrets lay hidden in the depths of that lake, condoms, unwanted pups, unwanted kittens sewn into sacks, and incriminating letters. In time, she would bring her own batch of letters, written on sleepless nights, some proud, some craven, all foolish, and assign them to this watery pyre.

She became more and more isolated, but the one person she did not shrink from was Ronan. He was a young man who lived in a caravan on the back avenue of the manor house where Mr and Mrs Jamieson lived. In return for being able to park there, he did odd jobs, cleared the woods, sawed timber, walked the greyhounds and lit the fires if the family was home of an evening. Now and then Mrs Jamieson gave her one of her husband's cast-offs but warned him not to let Sir know, as he was very sentimental about his belongings. Ronan and she made a pilgrimage together, for their special intentions, climbing up a steep mountain in Mayo, on a hot June day, with a busload of people who had been driven from the south. How relieved they both were that there was no one from their own vicinity, no one to spy on them. Often she wondered which of the locals had set upon the idea of torturing her with anonymous calls. They would come at all hours and always concerned Emmet, because Emmet was her lover's name, in honour of the hero Robert Emmet. Emmet, she would be told, had just got engaged to be married, Emmet was dating a dentist, Emmet was seen with a famous actress in Dublin, Emmet was seen in a shower with a brunette in a new spa in Westport. She knew they were lies, and yet to hear his name uttered and in such vile connotations, she longed to speak to him and warn him of these terrible calumnies.

It began to lessen. In her small gardens, one Sunday, she saw the stirrings of spring, the leaves of the camellia bush green and glossy, white buds, tight and tiny as birds' eggs, poised to open. She skimmed the sodden leaves from the rain barrel and standing there, looking, seeing, feeling the world around her, she realised that it was the commencement of her convalescence. A blackbird had found a luscious morsel of pink worm and was gobbling it, yet glancing left and right in case a fellow creature would snatch it away. Then, at the car boot sale, to which she went to pass the time, not one, but three different men smiled at her and she smiled back.

On the night when she gave herself to the minister, she believed, indeed knew, she had turned a corner. In their teens and while he was still a student, the minister and herself had met at a dance hall, had clicked and later sat in his motorcar, fondling and reciting poetry. She knew from the annual Christmas card down the years that he still remembered her and that he hankered in some way. When they found themselves at the same Summer school their joy at being reunited was immense. He was opening the event and she was giving a paper on the occult in Yeats's work. During the formal dinner, to which he had her invited, they exchanged glances, the odd word across the table, and eventually, not without a little detour, they found themselves in the same elevator and thence in his suite, which was so vast they had to grope their way to find a table lamp. Their lovemaking was at least twenty years too late, and they were too shy, lying in that enormous four poster bed, to laugh about it. At breakfast they were already on their separate ways, he to his house outside Dublin, and she further north, to the seat of the white mist.

She re-established friendships, went back to playing whist on Friday evenings and made a rhubarb jam flavoured with ginger, which she distributed among those who had been spiteful to her. Only Ronan knew. Ronan with his sideburns, dreaming of Elvis, of doing gigs in small towns, then graduating to big venues and finally to Dublin and afar. One night they watched a video of Elvis that she had hired, sitting in her front room by a warm fire and drinking red wine from the good cut glasses. There was Elvis, like a midnight God, in a midnight blue leather jacket and sideburns, wooing the world, Elvis asking a female member of the audience for the loan of her handkerchief to dab his brow, Elvis shivering as he half sang, half spoke, 'Are you lonesome tonight?' Ronan later strummed a song that he had written on his guitar, which he hoped would be a sensation at one of these imaginary gigs –

> Oh hollow heart you were so real
> I put my hand there
> I could feel
> Your hollow heart . . .

He looked at her, blinking – Ronan blinked out of nerves – and waited. She had to admit that it was not catchy enough and was somewhat bleak. Young people went to gigs to get high, to forget heartbreak and tedium.

'I can't do that . . . I can't forget,' Ronan said.

'Then don't,' Miss Gilhooley replied. But beyond that they did not dare go.

She came across her lover at a function a few years later, as she was wending her way through a room full of people, to table twenty-four. There was a priest with him and a young girl, perhaps his fiancée, though she could not tell. She stopped to say hello, not recalling a word of what was said, but she did and would remember how his arm, with a stealth, coming around the back of her waist and resting there for an instant, saying, without the words, what now would never be said. She drank somewhat immoderately at table twenty-four and kept repeating a line of Yeats's – 'A sweetheart from another life floats there' – much to the bafflement of the people around her.

At home she would mostly quell her desires, but when she went abroad in the summer, they ran amok. In that town on the Mediterranean, in stifling heat, everything quivered, even the knotted guaze scarves that swung from one of the stalls. The chrome of cars and motorcycles seemed to rasp in the head and in the jeweller's windows gold chains and gold wedding rings were at melting point. It was a crowded market, with a glut of goods – meats, fish, shellfish, fruits, vegetables, clothing, cutlery, handbags, seersucker skirts the colour of cotton candy, the locals knowing exactly what they had come for, steering their way with a certain pique through the loitering swell of visitors. The sun through the slits in the canvas awnings beat down relentlessly. A man wearing a faded blue shirt appeared as from nowhere and

slid between the milling crowd with a curious, knowing smile. He was dark-skinned, his left jaw showing
a strawberry mark, fiercely vivid, as if just slashed. He
stood right before her as if she had willed him there, the
encounter so thrilling and so unnerving, his eyes, which
were a soft brown, moist and lusting, asking her to say
yes. On one arm he carried a willow basket filled with
gardenias, the smell so intoxicating, adding to her flus-
ter and on the other arm there lay a snake, coiled and
inert, its scales iridescent in that hot light. She drew back
startled and he made some barely audible sound in order
to reassure her. And yes, she would have said yes, gone
down one of the narrow alleys, followed him to wherever he silently bade her, to lie with him. All that stopped
her was that her friend Amanda was nearby, trying on
different straw hats and beckoning her across. He took
the measure of the situation and sauntered off with the
ease of a panther.

The poet was late. The tall manageress blamed this late-
ness on the hopelessness of the train service. She herself
had been five hours getting home to her parents the
weekend previous.

'Where is home?' Miss Gilhooley asked.

'North east Galway,' she was told and tried to imagine
the little townlands on the big map in the library hall,
their names squeezed together in a cluster. After chatting
to Miss Gilhooley, the manageress insisted on bringing

one order of afternoon tea, saying that she would bring a second pot of tea when he arrived. She somehow guessed that it was a man. Presently a banquet was set before Miss Gilhooley – dainty sandwiches on white and brown bread, warm scones with helpings of clotted cream and raspberry jam, slices of rich fruitcake dense with raisins, currants, candied peel, cherries, and green strips of angelica and on the very top tier, as a final arpeggio, small gateaux of a sweet lemon flan, that trembled as the cake plate was put down. Except that she was not hungry.

She consulted her watch, regularly putting it to her ear to listen for the almost imperceptible ticking. A bellicose man at a centre table kept calling every other minute, to voice his complaints, addressing each of the passing waitresses as 'Serving person, Serving person.'

'An oddball . . . comes every day . . . lives alone somewhere in Ranelagh,' the manageress said, and hastened to his table, removing the cup and the saucer that was slopped with tea and speaking to him pleasantly.

People were munching and chatting, some consciously over-reserved, and from one table loud guffaws and peals of laughter at the richness of their jokes. She debated whether she should look, in the two bars and the Saddle room, but the truth was that she did not feel confident enough to wend her way past all those people. The heat in the room was now quite oppressive and a mobile phone rang repeatedly from the depths of someone's handbag. The pianist, sensible to the fact that he was being ignored, ran his hands along the keyboard with a flourish, then stood holding those self-same hands out, as for a requiem.

All of a sudden, she pictured her own hallway, with the storage heater about to come on and the radio playing full blast in the kitchen, a deliberate ploy, as there had been several break-ins in the town of late. The bellicose man was reading a newspaper, when suddenly he bashed his hand through the centre pages, shouting as obviously he had read something which infuriated him. His face was moist with rage and his ears, which were a blazing red, stuck out from his head as he looked around for an opponent to argue with. It was not at that precise moment that she admitted to herself that the poet was not coming. It was fifteen minutes later.

A little girl wearing a tam o'shanter came across and asked if she would care to buy a raffle ticket for an extension to be built at their school. As she wrote her address on the counterfoil, lest she came first, second, or third, the little girl rattled off the prizes, which were all of a culinary nature. As she walked off, her parents waved their gratitude and at that precise moment Miss Gilhooley put her arms back into the sleeves of her tweed coat, rising with as much composure as she could muster.

She paid at the cash register near the arched entrance and asked for the tip to be left on her table, as she dreaded the embarrassment of encountering the manageress, who was bound to be sympathetic.

Pat-the-Porter met her beaming. He had the booklet, the very last one, staff always swiping them, but he had it for her to take home as a souvenir. She mentioned the poet's name.

'Our Laureate,' he said, misquoting a line about a sod of earth rolling over on its back from the thrust of the plough.

'We had a . . . rendezvous,' she said, smarting at the pretentiousness of the word, and for a moment he was lost in perplexity, then drew her aside and in a low confidential voice began to mutter – 'Look . . . it's like this . . . I know the man . . . I can vouch for his honour . . . he comes here all the time with them bowsies . . . the bar-stool poets as I call them . . . and he sits like a man in a trance . . . he'd have every intention of meeting you . . . he'd want it . . . I can just see it . . . him shaving . . . putting on a clean shirt and tie, getting the good overcoat and setting out . . . coming as far as the corner by Wolfe Tone and all of a sudden . . . balking it.'

'But why . . . why would he balk it?'

'Shy, shyness . . . the shyest man I ever came across . . . I'll bet you he's walking the street now or maybe on a bench by the canal, reproaching himself for his blasted boorishness . . . his defection.'

It was left like that.

He steered her through the revolving doors and watched her go down the street. She held herself well, but there was a hurt look to her back.

The air in the bus was freezing, passengers not nearly so buoyant or talkative as they had been on the way down in the morning. She was glad that no one had sat next to her. In the various towns through which they passed, Paud, the young driver, drove with caution, because he had been stopped several times by the sergeant, but once onto the country roads he was reckless, the bus trundled, raising slush out of the ruts, grazing the hedges and twice coming to a skidding halt when a vehicle met them from the opposite side. Passengers were flung forward and afterwards there were irate calls to him 'For feck's sake, cool it, cool it.'

The dark seemed to get deeper and darker and the land itself swallowed within a primeval loneliness.

She had been dozing on and off, when suddenly, she came awake with a start. What an awful dream and where had it come from. She had been drinking the hot blood that spurted from the throat of a wounded animal, a wolf she reckoned. It was in a strange forest, the trunks of the trees massive and covered with white fleshy toadstools, a forest that was already receding from her mind, but the taste of blood lingered in her mouth. The horror. The horror. Was this the true her, a she-wolf drinking blood. Looking around, she sought in vain for deliverance, then wiped the window and saw that they were passing the low white building that had once been a creamery and was about twenty miles from home.

Home, the small town that so cried out for novelty

that a few fairy lights, since Christmas time, still dangled from the lower branches of the big chestnut tree in the market square, home to the loamy land and the brown-black lakes fed from bog water, home to the rooks convening and prattling at evening time in the churchyard grounds and home to the intangible white mist. Pressed to the window she said aloud the name of the man she had so loved, a name that had not passed her lips in almost twenty years, and all of a sudden she was crying, soft, warm, melting tears and she thought of the poet, that lonely clumsy man, walking streets in Dublin or, as Pat-the-Porter said, sitting on a bench staring into greenish canal water. She knew then, and with a cold conviction, the love, the desolation that goes in to the making of a poem.

'Welcome to Mullaghair . . . and all in one piece,' the grinning Paud said with Olympian pride.

People were slow to get down as the steps were slippery and so was the pavement, the goodnights were cursory and everyone, including her, drew up the collars of their coats, to guard against the biting wind.

My Two Mothers

In the dream, there is a kidney-shaped enamel spittoon, milk-white and a gleaming metal razor such as old-fashioned barbers use. My mother's hand is on the razor and then her face comes into view, swimming as it were towards me, pale, pear shaped, about to mete out its punishment, to cut the tongue out of me. Then with a glidingness the dream is over and I waken shaking, having escaped death not for the first time. In dream my mother and I are enemies, whereas in life we were so attached we could almost be called lovers. Yes, lovers insofar as I believed that the universe resided in her being.

She was the hub of the house, the rooms took on a life when she was in them and a death when she was absent. She was real mother and archetypal mother. Her fingers and her nails smelt of food – meal for hens and chickens, gruel for the calves and bread for us – whereas her body smelt of myriad things, depending on whether she was happy or unhappy, and the most pleasant was a lingering smell of a perfume from the cotton wad that she sometimes tucked under her brassiere. At Christmas time it was a smell of fruitcake soaked with grog and the sugary smell of white icing, stiff as starch, which she applied with the rapture of an artist.

Anything that had wonder attached to it was inevitably transposed onto her. For instance, when in the classroom one learned that our vast choppy lakes had the remains of cities buried beneath them, it seemed that in her, too, there were buried worlds. At mass, when the priest turned the key of the gold crested tabernacle door, I had the profane thought that he was turning a key in her chest. As if reading my mind she would pass her prayer book to me, solemn words in Latin, a language that neither of us was very conversant in.

We lived for a time in such a symbiosis that there might never have been a husband or other children, except that there were. We all sat at the same fire, ate the same food, and when a gift of a box of chocolates arrived looked with longing at a picture on the back, choosing our favourites in our minds. That box might not be opened for a year. Life was frugal and unpredictable, the harvests and the ripening hay subject to the hazards of rain and ruin. Hovering over us there was always the spectre of debt. Yet in our house, there were touches of grandeur – silver cloches that resembled the helmets of medieval knights stationed along the bog-oak sideboard, and mirrors encrusted with cupids kissing and cuddling. In drawers upstairs were folds of silk from the time when she worked long before, in the silk department of a department store in Brooklyn, the name of which ranked second only to Heaven. On Sundays for mass, she would hurriedly don her good clothes that had been

acquired in those times, or later, cast-offs sent by relatives, voile dresses cut on the bias that seemed to sway
over a body, over hers. I would beg of her to re-don them
in the evening so that we could go for a walk, and in
summer at least enjoy the evening intoxication of stock
in other people's gardens.

We had an orchard, ploughed fields and meadows.
Somehow I thought that a garden would be a prelude
to happiness. The only flowers I had occasion to study
were those painted on china cups and plates, splotches
of gentian in cavities of moss, and on the wallpaper
tinted rosebuds so compact, so life-like, one felt that one
could squeeze or crush them. Those walks bordered on
enchantment, what with neighbours in some sudden
comraderie, greeting us profusely, and always, iration-
ally, the added possibility that we might walk out of our
old sad existence. She was beautiful. She had beautiful
hair, brown with bronzed glimmers in it, and blue-blue
eyes that held within them an infinite capacity for stric-
ture. To chastise one she did not have to speak – her eyes
did it with a piercing gaze. But when she approved of
something, everything seemed to soften and the gaze,
intensely blue, was like seeing a stained-glass window
melt.

On those walks she invariably spoke of visitors that
were bound to come in the summer and the dainty dishes she would prepare for them. There was a host of reci-
pes she had not yet tried. Sometimes her shoes hurt and

we had to sit on a wall while she rolled down her stockings and mashed and massaged her poor reddened toes.
Once, a man that we scarcely knew came and sat down
beside us. He wore a torn flannel shirt and spoke in a
wild voice, kept asking us 'Any news . . . any news'. She
laughed over it afterwards and said he was a bostoon. I
secretly thought she would have liked a city life, a life
where she could wear those good clothes and her rar-
eified Sunday court shoes with their stout buckles. Yet
at heart she was a country woman, and as she got older
the fields, the bog, her dogs, and her fowl became more
important to her, were her companions once I had left. I
had always promised not to leave. I promised it aloud to
her and alone to myself as I looked at the silver knights
on the sideboard and the about-to-burst rosebuds in the
wallpaper.

Our house had quarrels in it, quarrels about money,
about drinking, about recklessness, but not content with
real fear she also had to summon up the unknown and
the supernatural. A frog jumped into the fire one night
and she believed it was the augury for the sudden and
accidental death of a neighbour. Likewise a panel of coloured glass above a vestibule door broke again and again,
and she insisted that it was not wind or storm but a message from beyond. One evening, sitting in the kitchen
in some dread, she conceived the thought that a man, a
stranger, had come and stood outside the window pre-
paring to shoot us. We moved to the side of the window

and sat on two kitchen chairs, barely breathing, waiting for our executioner. We sat there till morning, when her husband, who had been gone for days, appeared, unslept, still half drunk and vexed at having to return to us. She and I were mendicants together – cooking, making beds, folding sheets, doing all the normal things in the so-called normal times, and in opposite times cowering out of doors, under trees, our teeth chattering in mad musical shudder. We were inseparable.

I cannot remember when exactly the first moment of the breach came. There were tiffs over food that I refused to eat and disapproval about gaudy slides that I put in my hair. I began to write – jottings that had to be covert because she would see in them a sort of wanderlust. She insisted that literature was a precursor to sin and damnation, whereas I believed it was the only alchemy that there was. I would read and I would write and she, the adjudicator of what I was writing, had to be banished, just as in a fairy tale. One day she lost her temper completely when I read aloud to her a quotation of Voltaire's that I had copied – 'Illusion is the queen of the human heart'. She looked at me as if I had escaped from the lunatic asylum twenty miles away.

'Illusion, queen of the human heart,' she said, and went on with her task. She was pounding very yellow oatmeal with boiling water, and the vehemence with which she did it was so great she might have been pounding me. Those passions, those sentiments that were in Voltaire or in Tolstoy, the recklessness of a Natasha willing to elope with a cad through a window, those were the heights I now aspired to. She sensed the impulse in me the way a truffle hound sniffs the spoils buried beneath, and a current of mistrust sprang up between us.

She searched my eyes, she searched my clothing, she searched my suitcase when as a student I returned home from Dublin – the few books I had brought with me she deemed foul and degenerate. The battle was on, but we skirted around it. I wrote and she silently seethed. She would tell me what others – neighbours – thought of what I wrote, tears in her voice at my criminality. Flings, youthful love affairs were out of the question, yet I threw my lot in with a man I had only known for six weeks. Though hating him by merely seeing a photograph of him, she nevertheless insisted on my marrying to give the seal of respectability to things and there followed a bleak ceremony, which she did not attend. With uncanny clairvoyance she predicted the year, the day, even the hour of its demise. Ten years and two children later, when it happened, she wrote her ultimatum. It was sent post-restante and I read it in a street in London. She enjoined me to kneel down on the very spot as I was reading and make the vow to have nothing to do with any man in body or soul as long as I lived, adding that I owed it to God, to her, and to my children. She lamented the fact of my being young and therefore still in the way of temptation. She had reclaimed me.

Then came years and years of correspondence from her. She who professed disgust at the written word wrote daily, bulletins that ranged from the pleading to the poetic, the philosophic, and the commonplace. I never fully read them, being afraid of some greater accusation, and my replies were little niceties, squeezed in with bribes and money to stave off confrontation. Yet there was something that I wanted to ask her about. I sensed the secret inside her. An infant before me had been born prematurely and had died, and I believed it was caused by some drastic transaction between the two of them. Why else was its name never uttered, prayers for it never said, and never did we visit the grave where even the four letters of its name were not inscribed on the tombstone underneath that of distant forebears. She had not wanted another child, three children and waning finances were hardship enough, and by being born two years later I had in some way usurped her will.

For twenty-odd years I had postponed opening the bundle of letters that lay in my house, in a leather trunk, enjoinders that I had not read and had not the heart to destroy. Then one day, deluding myself into the belief that I needed for my work to revisit rooms and haunts that had passed into other hands, I lifted the little brass latch and took them out. It was like being plunged into the moiling seas of memory. Her letters were deeper, sadder than I had remembered, but what struck me most was their hunger and their thirst. Here was a woman desperately trying to explain herself and to be understood. There were hundreds of them, or maybe a thousand. They came two, three a week, always with apology for not having written in the intervening days. I read them and stowed them away. She would wonder whether I was at home or away, wonder how soon we would meet again, wonder what new clothes I had got, or any other extravagant item of furniture. She would swear to cross the sea to England, even if she had to walk it, and slyly I postponed these visits. She would send things from her linen press, and the letter which preceded the parcel read – 'I sent you yesterday eighteen large doyleys, eighteen small ones and four central ones . . . I didn't get to wash and starch them as it takes so long to iron them properly, when starched.' The next letter or the one following would be about toil. She had drawn one hundred buckets of water and sprayed the entire avenue with weedkiller to kill off the nettles. One Sunday she had gone for a walk, further than she had ever gone before. It was a scorching day, as she said, and she felt a strange kind of energy, an exhilaration as when she was young. Up there on the slopes of the mountain there were ripe blackberries, masses of them on the briars, and not wishing to have them rot she began to pick them to make blackberry jelly. Without basket or can, she had to remove her slip and put the blackberries inside it where they shed some of their purple juices. Her letter kept wishing that she could hand me a pot of clear jelly over a hedge and see me taste and swallow it.

I had no intention of going back to buy a house or a plot of land, but nevertheless she had her eye out for holdings that might suit me. One was called Gore House, named after an English landlord, long since dead. She said it was a pity I had not bought it instead of the German clothier, who not only never set foot in it but had bought it when he saw it from the air, travelling in his private jet. Continentals loved the place and therefore why not I?

The letters about her dogs were the most wrenching. She always had two dogs, sheep dogs, who sparred and growled at one another throughout the day, apart from when they were off hunting rabbits, but who at night slept more or less in each other's embrace, like big honey-coloured bears. They were named Laddie and Rover and always met with the same fate. They had a habit of following cars in the avenue and one, either one, got killed while the other grieved and mourned, refused food, even refused meat, as she said – kept listening to the sounds of dogs barking in the distance, and in a short time died and was buried with its comrade. She would swear never to get another pair of dogs, but yet in a matter of months she was writing off to a breeder several counties away and two little puppies in a cardboard box, couched in a nest of dank straw, would arrive by bus and presently be given the identical names of Laddie and Rover. She gloried in describing how mischievous they were, the things they ate, pranks they were up to. She looked out one May morning and thought it was snowing, but when she went outdoors she found that they had bitten the sheets off the clothes line, chewed small pieces and spat them out.

Her life got increasingly harder – there were floods and more floods, and heating-oil got costlier each year while the price of cattle went rock bottom. People were killing their own beef, but as she said for that one needed a deep freezer, which she did not have. A mare that my father loved and had despatched to a trainer was expected to come first in a big race but merely came third, and the difference in the booty was that of a few pounds as opposed to several hundred pounds, thereby crushing all hopes of riches. The mare could have come first but that she was temperamental – could be last in a race, then out of the blue pass them all out or purposely lag behind. Not having the means, she nevertheless lived for the day when she could afford to get me a chandelier and to have it so carefully wrapped that not a single crystal would get broken. I did not have that much of a wish for a chandelier.

As she got older she admitted to being tired and sometimes the letters were in different inks where she had stopped writing or maybe had fallen asleep. Death was now the big factor, the six-mark question that could not be answered. She was bewildered. She began to have doubts about her faith. One morning for several moments

she went blind, and from that day onwards she hated
night and hated dark and said she lay awake fearing that
dawn would never come. Life, she maintained, was one
big battle, because no matter who wins nobody does. I
began to see her in a new light and resolved to clear up
the differences between us, get rid of the old grudges and
regain the tenderness we once had. I always pictured her
at work, removing the clinkers from the ash pan in the
morning and separated them from the half-burnt knobs
of anthracite, which she mixed in with the good stuff as
an economy. She loved that Aga cooker that was kept
on all night, because formerly it was a hearth fire that
would have to be quenched and had to be coaxed with
balls of newspaper, sugar and paraffin oil. I realised that
what I admired in her most was her unceasing labour,
allowing for no hour of rest, no day of rest. She had set
me an example by her resilience and a strange childish
gratitude for things.

She began, as things grew darker, to implicitly forgive
my transgressions, whatever they might have been. I was
going to America and she asked me to track down a gentleman at an address in Brooklyn. He must have been
a sweetheart. She believed that it had been opened and
therefore read. It was like finding a hidden room in a
house I thought I knew. I remembered something that as
a child I had blushed at overhearing. We were in a hire
car – my mother, a newly married woman called Lydia,
and myself – waiting outside a hospital for a coffin to

be brought out to the hearse. My father and the driver had gone inside. Lydia chain smoked, laughed a lot, and was vibrantly happy. My mother was delighted that we had given her a lift and began to get talkative. Normally guarded with neighbours, my mother began to tell this stranger of her glorious time in Brooklyn, the style she had, the dances she went to, the men she met. Pressed on that point, she said that yes there was one in particular, dark, handsome, and with a beautiful reserve. He had been such a gentleman, had given her little gifts, and on their Sunday outings had seen her back home to her digs and shook her hand on the doorstep. Yet one night, passing a house of ill repute with its red lights and its sumptuous velvet curtains, he had nudged her and said that maybe they should go in there and see what went on. She did not say if the friendship had been broken off abruptly but it was clear from a little shiver in her body in which desire and disgust overlapped, that she had probably loved him and wished that she could have gone through that forbidden door with him.

Even as I was resolving to go to that address in Brooklyn she was taken ill at home and driven to a hospital in the city, hundreds of miles away. Like many another in a time of reckoning, she decided that she wished to change her will with regard to her house, which had for her the magic of a doll's house. She wished to give it to me. Her son, hearing that he was about to be disinherited, came in high dudgeon and they quarrelled in the gaunt hospital hall. She got into some sort of fit there and was brought back to bed, her mind rambling. Late in the evening she began her last letter – 'my hand is shaking now as well as myself with what I have to tell you'.

It remains unfinished, which is why I wait for the dream that leads us beyond the ghastly white spittoon and the metal razor, to fields and meadows, up onto the mountain, that bluish realm, half earth, half sky, towards her dark man, to begin our journey all over again, to live our lives as they should have been lived, happy, trusting, and free of shame.

Old Wounds

In our front garden, there were a few clumps of devil's pokers – spears of smouldering crimson when in bloom, and milky yellow when not. But my mother's sister and her family, who lived closer to the mountain, had a ravishing garden: tall festoons of pinkish-white roses, a long low border of glorious golden tulips, and red dahlias that, even in hot sun, exuded the coolness of velvet. When the wind blew in a certain direction, the perfume of the roses vanquished the smell of dung from the yard, where the sow and her young pigs spent their days foraging and snortling. My aunt was so fond of the piglets that she gave each litter pet names, sometimes the same pet names, which she appropriated from the romance novels she borrowed from the library and read by the light of a paraffin lamp, well into the night.

Our families had a falling out. For several years there was no communication between us at all, and, when the elders met at funerals, they did not acknowledge one another and studiously looked the other way. Yet we were still intimately bound up with each other and any news of one family was of interest to the other, even if that news was disconcerting.

When the older and possibly more begrudging people had died off, and my cousin Edward and I were both past middle age – as he kept reminding me, he was twelve years older than I was and had been fitted with a pacemaker – we met again and set aside the lingering hostilities. About a year later, we paid a visit to the family graveyard, which was on an island in the broad stretch of the Shannon River. It was a balmy day in autumn, the graveyard spacious, uncluttered, the weathered tombs far more imposing than those in the graveyard close to the town. They were limestone tombs, blotched with white lichen, great splashes of it, which lent an improvised gaiety to the scene. Swallows were swooping and scudding in and out of the several sacred churches, once the abode of monks but long since uninhabited, the roofs gone but the walls and ornamental doorways still standing, grey and sturdy, with their own mosaics of lichen. The swallows did not so much sing as caw and gabble, their circuits a marvel of speed and ingenuity.

Now I was seeing the graveyard in daylight with my cousin, but once, a few years before, I had gone there surreptitiously. The youngster who rowed me across worked for a German man who bred pheasants on one of the other islands and was able to procure a boat. We set out just before dark. The boy couldn't stop talking or singing. And he smoked like a chimney.

'Didn't yer families fight?' he asked, when I trained a torch on the names of my ancestors carved on a tall headstone. Undaunted by my silence, the boy kept prying and then, with a certain insouciance, informed me that the family fight had come about because of what Edward had done to his widowed mother, flinging her out once she had signed the place over to him.

'That's all in the past,' I said curtly, and recited the names, including those of a great-grandmother and a great-grandfather, a Bridget and a Thomas, of whom I knew nothing. Others I had random remembrances of. In our house, preserved in a china cabinet, on frayed purple braid, were the medals of an uncle who had been a soldier of the Irish Free State and had met with a violent death, aged twenty-eight. I remembered my grandfather falling into a puddle in the yard, when he came home drunk from a fair, and laughing jovially. My grandmother was stern and made me drink hot milk with pepper before sending me up to bed early. She was forever dinning into me the stories of our forebears and how they had suffered, our people driven from their holdings and their cabins down the years. She said that the knowledge of eviction and the fear of the poorhouse ran in our blood. I must have been seven or eight at the time. For Sunday Mass, she wore a bonnet made of black satin, with little felt bobbins that hopped against her cheek in the judder, as my grandfather drove helter-skelter so as not to be late. The traps and the sidecars were tethered outside the chapel gates, and the horses seemed to know one another and to nod lazily. As a treat, my grandmother let me smell a ball of nutmeg, which was kept in a round tin that had once held cough pastilles. The feather bed, which I shared with her, sagged almost to the floor and the pillow slips smelt of flour, because they were made from flour bags that she had bleached and sewn. My grandfather, who snored, slept in a settle bed down in the kitchen, near the fire.

About two years after my clandestine visit to the grave-yard, Edward and I met by chance at a garden centre. I was home on holiday and had gone to buy broom shrubs for my nephew. As we approached each other on a path-way between a line of funereal yew trees, my cousin saw me, then pretended not to and feigned interest in a huge tropical plant, behind which, he slid. Deciding to brave it, I said his name, and, turning, he asked with a puz-zled look, 'Who do I have here?', although he well knew. And so the ice was broken. Yes, his eyes were bad, as he later told me, but he had indeed recognised me and felt awkward. As we got to be friends, I learned of the journeys to the eye doctor in Dublin, of the treatments required before the doctor could operate, and when I sent him flowers at the hospital the nurse, bearing them to his bedside, said, 'Well, someone loves you,' and he was proud to tell her that it was me.

We corresponded. His letters were so immedi-ate. They brought that mountain terrain to life, along with the unvarying routine of his days: out to the fields straight after breakfast, herding, mending fences, fixing gates, clearing drains, and often, as he said, sitting on a wall for a smoke, to drink in his surroundings. He loved the place. He said that people who did not know the country – did not know nature and did not stay close to it – could never understand the loss that they were feeling. I felt that, in an oblique way, he was referring to me. He wrote these letters at night by the fire, after his wife had gone up to bed. Her health was poor, her sleep fitful, so she went to bed early to get as many hours as she could. He sometimes, while writing, took a sup of whiskey, but he said he was careful not to get too fond of it.

He knew the lake almost as well as he knew the mountain, and, through his binoculars, from his front porch he watched the arrival of the dappers in the month of May, a whole fleet of boats from all over the country and even from foreign parts. They arrived as the hatched mayflies came out of the nearby bushes and floated above the water, in bacchanalian swarms, so that the fishermen were easily able to catch them and fix them to the hooks of their long rods. He himself had fished there every Sunday of his life, trolling from his boat with wet or dry bait, and so canny was he that the neighbours were quite spiteful, saying that he knew exactly where the fish lay hiding, and, hence, there was not a pike or a perch or a trout left for anyone else.

He was a frugal man. In Dublin, he would walk miles from the railway station to the eye hospital, often having to ask the way and frequently going astray because of his ailing sight. His wife and son would scold him for not taking a taxi, to which he always said, 'I could if I wanted to.' Yet I recalled that time when, young, he had brought my sister and me a gift, the same gift, a red glassy bracelet on an elasticated band. The raised red beads were so beautiful that I licked them as I would jellies. My sister was older than me, and it was for her that he had a particular fondness. They flirted, though I did not know then that it was called that. They teased each other, and then ran around the four walls of our sandstone house, and eventually fell into an embrace, breathless from their hectic exertions. I was wild with jealousy and snapped on the band of my new bracelet. They aped dancing, as if in a ballroom, she swooning, her upper back reclining on the curve of his forearm as he sang, 'You'll be lonely, little sweetheart, in the spring,' and she gazed up at him, daring him to kiss her. He was handsome then, not countrified, like most of the farmers or their grown sons, and he wore a long white belted motor coat. He had a mop of silky brown hair, and his skin was sallow.

I met Moira, the woman to whom he got engaged some two or three years later, on the way home from school one day. She stopped me and asked if I was his cousin, though she knew well who I was and pointedly ignored the two girls who were with me. She asked me jokingly if she was making the right choice, as someone had warned her that my cousin was 'bad news'. She repeated the words 'bad news' with a particular relish. She was wearing a wraparound red dress and red high-heeled toeless sandals, which looked incongruous but utterly beautiful on that dusty godforsaken road. She was like flame, a flame in love with my cousin, and her eyes danced with mischief. It was not long after they got married that he called his mother out into the hay shed and informed her that his wife felt unwanted in the house and that, for the sake of his marriage, he had to ask her to leave. Thus the coolness from our side of the family. There was general outrage in the parish that an only son had pitched his mother out, and pity for the mother, who had to walk down that road, carrying her few belongings and her one heirloom, a brass lamp with a china shade, woebegone, like a woman in a ballad. She stayed with us for a time, and did obliging things for my mother, being, as she was, in her own eyes, a mendicant, and once, when she let fall a tray of good china cups and saucers, she knelt down and said, 'I'll replace these,' even though we knew she couldn't. In the evenings, she often withdrew from the kitchen fire to sit alone in our cold vacant room, with a knitted shawl over her shoulders, brooding. Eventually, she rented a room in the town, and my mother gave her cane chairs, cushions, and a pale-green candlewick bedspread, to give the room a semblance of cheer.

But, with so many dead, there was no need for estrangement anymore.

Edward sent me a photograph of a double rainbow, arc-

ing from the sky above his house across a patchwork of
small green fields and over the lake toward the hill that
contained the graves of the Leinster men. On the back
of the photograph he had written the hour of evening
at which the rainbow had appeared and lasted for about
ten minutes, before eking its watery way back into the
sky. I put it on the mantelpiece for luck. The rainbow,
with its seven bands of glorious colour, always presaged
happiness. In his next letter and in answer to my question, he said that the Leinster men were ancient chief-
tains who had come for a banquet in Munster, where
they were insulted and subsequently murdered, but in a
remaindered gesture of honour someone had thought to
bury them facing their own province.

Each summer, when I went back to Ireland, we had
outings, outings that he had been planning all year. One
year, mysteriously, I found that we were driving far
from his farm, up an isolated road, with nothing in sight
except clumps of wretched rushes and the abandoned
ruins from famine times. Then, almost at the peak, he
parked the jeep and took two shotguns out of the boot.
He had dreamed all year of teaching me to shoot and he
set about it with a zest. He loved shooting. As a youngster, unbeknownst to his mother, he had cycled to Limerick two nights a week to learn marksmanship in a gal-
lery. With different gundogs, he shot pheasants, grouse,
ducks and snipe, but his particular favourites were the
woodcock, which came all the way from Siberia or Cher-

nobyl. He described them to me, silhouetted against an evening sky – they disliked light – their beaks like crochet hooks, then furtively landing in a swamp or on a cowpat to catch insects or partake of the succulence of the water. Yet he could not forgo the thrill of shooting them, then picking them up, feeling the scant flesh on the bone, and snapping off a side feather to post to an ornithologist in England. September 1st, he said, was the opening of duck shooting on the lake, a hundred guns or more out there, *bang-bang*ing in all directions. Later, adjourning to the pub, the sportsmen swapped stories of the day's adventure, comparing what they'd shot and how they'd shot and what they'd missed – a conviviality such as he was not used to.

For a target, he affixed a saucepan lid to a wooden post. Then, taking the lighter of the two guns, he loaded it with brass bullets, handed it to me, and taught me to steady it, to put my finger on the trigger and look down through the nozzle of the long blue-black barrel.

'Now shoot,' he said in a belligerent voice, and I shot so fearfully and, at the same time, so rapidly that I believed I was levitating. The whole thing felt unreal, bullets bursting and zapping through the air, some occasionally clattering off the side of the tin lid and my aim so awry that even to him it began to be funny. He had started to lay out a picnic on a tartan rug – milky tea in a bottle, hard-boiled eggs, slices of brown bread already buttered – when out of thin air a huge black dog appeared, like a phantom or an animal from the underworld, its snarls strange and spiteful. Its splayed paws were enormous and mud-splattered, its eyes bloodshot, the sockets bruised, as if it were fresh from battle.

'He'll smell your fear,' my cousin said.

'I can't help it,' I said and lowered the gun, thinking that this might, in some way, appease the animal. There wasn't a stone or a stick to throw at it. There was nothing up there, only the fearsome dog and us and the saucepan lid rattling like billio.

Edward knew every dog for miles around, and every breed of dog, and said that this freak was a 'blow-in'. Eventually, he sacrificed every bit of food in order to get the animal to run, throwing each piece further and further as matador-like he followed, bearing the stake on which the lid was nailed, shouting in a voice that I could not believe was his, so barbaric and inhuman did it sound. The dog, wearying of the futility of this, decided to gallop off over the edge of the mountain and disappear from sight.

'Jesus,' my cousin said.

We sat in the jeep because, as he said, we were in no hurry to get home. We didn't talk about family things, his wife or my ex-husband, my mother or his mother, possibly fearing that it would open up old wounds. There had been so many differences between the two families – over greyhounds, over horses, over some rotten bag of seed potatoes – and always with money at the root of it. My father, in his wild tempers, would claim that my mother's father had not paid her dowry and would go to his house in the dead of night, shouting up at a window to demand it.

Instead we talked of dogs.

Having been a huntsman all his life, Edward had several dogs, good dogs, faithful dogs, retrievers, pointers, setters and springers. His favourite was an Irish red setter, which he called Maire Ruadh, for a red-haired noblewoman who had her husbands pitched into the Atlantic once she tired of them. He had driven all the way to Kildare, in answer to an advertisement, to vet this pedigree dog, and his wife had decided to come along. Straightaway they had liked the look of her; they had studied the pedigree papers, paid out a hefty sum, and there and then given her her imperious name. On the way back, they'd had high tea at a hotel in Roscrea, and, what with the price he'd paid for Maire Ruadh and the tea and the cost of the petrol, it had proved to be an expensive day.

I told him the story of an early morning in a café in Paris, a straggle of people – two men, each with a bottle of pale-amber beer, and a youngish woman, writing in a ruled copybook, her dog at her feet, quiet, suppliant. When she finished her essay, or whatever it was that she had been writing, she groped in her purse and all of a sudden the obedient dog reared to get away. She pulled on the lead, dragging it back beside her, the dog resistant and down on its haunches. Grasping the animal by the crown of its head, she opened its mouth very wide and with her other hand dispatched some powdered medicine from a sachet onto its tongue. Pinned as it was, the dog could vent its fury only by kicking, which got it nowhere. Once the dog had downed the powder, she patted it lovingly and it answered in kind, with soft whimpers.

'Man's best friend,' my cousin said, a touch dolefully.

We came back by a different route because he wanted me to see the ruin of a cottage where a workman of ours had lived. As a child, I had been dotingly in love with the man and had intended to elope with him, when I came of age. The house itself was gone and all that remained was a tumbledown porch with some overgrown stalks of geranium, their scarlet blooms prodigal in that godforsaken place. We didn't even get out of the car. Yet nearby we came upon a scene of such gaiety that it might have been a wedding party. Twenty or so people sitting out of doors at a long table strewn with lanterns, eating, drinking, and calling for toasts in different tongues. Behind the din of voices we could hear the strains of music from a melodeon. It was the hippies who had come to the district, the 'blow-ins', as Edward called them, giving them the same scathing name as the fearsome dog. They had made Ireland their chosen destination when the British government, in order to avoid paying them social benefits, gave them a lump sum to scoot it. They crossed the Irish Sea and found ideal havens by streams and small rivers, building houses, growing their own vegetables and their own marijuana, and, he had been told on good authority, taking up wife-swapping. He had the native's mistrust of the outsider. We had to come to a stop because some of their ducks were waddling across the road. We couldn't see them in the dusk but heard their quacking, and then some children with their faces painted puce came to the open window of the jeep, holding lighted sods of turf, serenading us.

'Hi, guv,' one of the men at the table called out, but my cousin did not answer.

It was in his back yard, still sitting in the jeep, that he began to cry. As we drove in, he could see by the light in the upstairs room that his wife had gone to bed early, so I declined his invitation to have a cup of tea. He cried for a long time. The stars were of the same brightness and fervour as the stars I had seen in childhood and, though distant, seemed to have been put there for us, as if someone in the great house called Heaven had gone from room to room, turning on this constellation of lamps. He was crying, he said, because the families had been divided for so long. He had even tried to find me in England, had written to some priest who served in a parish in Kilburn, because, according to legend, Kilburn was where Irish people flocked and had fights on Saturday nights outside pubs and pool halls. The priest couldn't trace me but suggested a parish in Wimbledon, where I had indeed lived for a time, before fleeing from bondage. What hurt my cousin most was the fact that his wife's cousins, as she frequently reminded him, had kept in touch, had sent Christmas cards and visited in the summer, each of them rewarded with a gift of a pair of fresh trout. In his wife's estimation, his cousins, meaning my family, were heartless. It took him a while to calm down. The tissues that he took from his pockets were damp shreds. Eventually, somewhat abashed, he said, 'Normally, I am not an emotional man,' then, backing the car toward the open gate, he drove down the mountain road to the small town where my nephew lived.

One evening soon after that, when I telephoned him from London, he said that he had known it would be me; he had come in from the fields ten minutes before the Angelus tolled, because of this hunch he had that I would be ringing. We talked of recent things: the cornea transplant he had undergone, a robbery in a house further up the mountain, where an old man was tied with rope, the weather as ever wet and squally. He told me that it was unlikely he would make silage anymore and therefore intended to sell the cattle that he had fattened all summer. He might, he said, buy yearlings the following May, if his health held up. He did not say how happy the call had made him, but I could feel the pitch of excitement in his voice as he told me again that he had come in early from the fields because he knew that I would ring.

We took to talking on the phone about once a month. When his wife went to Spain with their son, from whom he was estranged, he wrote to tell me that he would phone me on a particular evening at seven o'clock. I knew then that these conversations buoyed him up.

It was the third summer of our reunion, and he had the boat both tarred and painted a Prussian blue. We were bound for the graveyard. The day could not have been more perfect: sunshine, a soft breeze, Edward slipping the boat out with one oar through a thicket of lush bamboo and reeds, a scene that could easily have taken place somewhere in the tropics. He took a loop away from the direction of the island, in order to get the breeze at our backs, then turned on the engine and, despite his worsening sight, steered with unfailing instinct, because he had, he said, a map of the entire lake inside his head. The water was a lacquered silver, waves barely nudging the boat. We couldn't hear each other because of the noise of the engine but sat quiet, content, the hills all around sloping toward us, enfolding us in their friendliness. It was only when we reached the pier that I realised how poor his sight was – by the difficulty he had tying the rope to its ballast and his having to ask me to read the handwritten sign on a piece of cardboard, nailed to a tree-trunk, that said 'Bull on island'.

'We'll have to brave it,' he said. Our headway was cautious, what with the steep climb, the fear of the bull, and, presently, a herd of bullocks fixing us with their stupid glare, and a few of them making abortive attempts to charge at us. Once through the lych-gate that led to the graveyard, we sat and availed ourselves of the port wine that I had brought in a hip flask. Sitting on the low wall opposite the resting place of our ancestors, he said what a pity it was that my mother had chosen not to be buried there. Her explanation was that she wished to be near a roadside so that passers-by might bless themselves for the repose of her soul, but I had always felt that there was another reason, a hesitation in her heart.

'I came here twice since I last saw you . . . to think,' he said.

'To think?'

'I was feeling rotten . . . I came here and talked to them.' He did not elaborate, but I imagined that he might have been brooding over unfinished business with his mother, or maybe his marriage, which had grown bleaker amid the desolations of age. It was not money he was worried about, because, as he told me, he had been offered princely sums for fields of his that bordered the lake; people were pestering him, developers and engaged couples, to sell them sites, and he had refused resolutely.

'My wants are few,' he said and rolled a cigarette, regaining his good humour and rejoicing at the fact that we had picked such a great day for our visit. He surprised me by telling a story of how, after my mother died, my father had gone to the house of Moira's older sister, Oonagh, recently returned from Australia and had proposed to her. Without any pretence at courtship, he had simply asked her to marry him. He had needed a wife. He had even pressed her to think it over, then narked at her refusal, he had gone on the batter for several weeks. I could not imagine anyone other than my mother in our kitchen, in our upstairs or downstairs rooms; she was the presiding spirit of the place.

He then said that Moira had also expressed a wish to be buried in a grave near the town and he could not understand why anyone would want to be in a place where the remains were squeezed in like sardines.

Birds whirled in and out, such a freedom to their movements, such an airiness, as if the whole place belonged to them and we were the intruders. He spoke of souls buried there in pagan times, then Christian times, the monks in the monasteries fasting, praying, and most likely having to fend off invaders. It was a place of pilgrimage, where all-night Masses were celebrated; he pointed to boulders with little cavities, where the pilgrims had dipped their hands and their feet in the blessed water.

'Hallowed ground,' I said. The grassy mound that covered our family grave was a rich warm green strewn with speckled wildflowers.

'You have as much right to be there as I have,' he said suddenly, and my heart leaped with a childish joy.

'Do I really?'

'I'm telling you . . . you'll be right beside me,' he said, and he stood up and took my hand, and we walked over the mound, measuring it, as it were, hands held in solidarity. It meant everything to me. I would be the only one from our branch of the family to lie with relatives whom I had always admired as being more stoic than us and closer to the land.

When his wife got sick the next winter, his letters became infrequent. He rarely went out to the fields, having to tend her, and the only help was a twice-weekly visit from a jubilee nurse, who came to change her dressings. They could not tell whether it was the cancer causing all the wounds down her spine or whether she was allergic to the medicines that she had been prescribed. Sometimes, he wrote, she roared with pain, said that the pain was hammering against her chest, and begged to be dead. I was abroad when she died and he telephoned to let me know. A message was passed on to me and I was able to send roses by Interflora. To my surprise, I learned that she had been buried on the island after all, and on the phone, when I later spoke to him, he described the crossing of the funeral procession, the first boat for the flowers, as was the custom, then himself and his son in the next boat, and the mourners following behind.

'A grand crowd . . . good people,' he said, and I realised that he was vexed with me for not having been there. I asked whether she had died suddenly, and he answered that he would rather not describe the manner of her passing. Nor did he say why she had changed her mind about being buried in the family plot.

I could not tell what had caused it, but a chasm had sprung up between us. The friendliness had gone from his voice when I rang, and his letters were formal now. I wondered if he felt that his friendship with me had somehow compromised his love for his wife, or if he was in the grip of that spleen which comes, or so I feared, with advancing years. A home help, a very young girl, visited him three days a week, put groceries in the fridge, cooked his dinner, and occasionally went upstairs to hoover and change the sheets.

'Maybe you should give her a bonus,' I said, suggesting that she would then come every day.

'The state pays her plenty,' he said, disgruntled by my remark.

I got out of the habit of phoning him, but one Christmas morning, in a burst of sentiment, I rang, hoping that things might be smoothed over. Over-politely, he answered a few questions about the weather, his health, a large magnifying machine that he had got for reading, and then quite suddenly he blurted it out. He had been looking into the cost of a tombstone for his wife and himself and had found that it was going to be very expensive.

'Have you thought of what you intend to do?' he asked.

'I haven't,' I said flatly.

'Maybe you would like to purchase yours now,' he said.

'I don't understand the question,' I said, although I understood it all too clearly and a river of outrage ran through me. I felt that he had violated kinship and decency. The idea of being interred in the graveyard beside him seemed suddenly odious to me. Yet, perversely, I was determined not to surrender my place under the grassy slope.

There were a few seconds of wordless confrontation and then the line went dead. He had hung up. I rang back, but the telephone was off the hook, and that night, when I called again, there was no answer; he probably guessed that it was me.

It was August and pouring rain when I travelled to the local hospital to see him. A nurse, with her name tag, 'M. Gleeson', met me in the hallway. She was a stout woman with short bobbed hair and extremely affable. She eyed me up and down, guessed correctly whom I had come to see, and said that her mother had known me well, but, of course, I wouldn't remember, being a toff. If my cousin had come in at Easter, things might have been different now, she said, but, as it was, the news was not promising.

'How's the humour?' I asked tentatively.

'Cantankerous,' she said, adding that most patients knew their onions, knew how to play up to her, realising that she would be the one to wash them, feed them, and bring them cups of tea at all hours, but not cousin Edward.

'I should have brought flowers,' I said.

'Ah, aren't you flower enough!' she said and herded me toward the open door of his little room, announcing me bluffly.

He was in an armchair with a fawn dressing gown over his pyjamas, as thin as a rake, his whole body drooping, and when he looked up and saw me, or perhaps only barely saw me, but heard my name, his eyes narrowed with hatred. I saw that I should not have come.

'I couldn't find anywhere to buy you a flower,' I said.

'A flower?' he said with disdain.

'They don't sell them in the garden centre anymore – only trees and plants,' I explained, and the words hung in the air. The rain sloshed down the narrow windowpane as if it couldn't reach the sill quickly enough, then overflowed onto a patch of ground that was smothered with nettle and dock.

'How are you?' I asked after some time.

He pondered the question and then replied, coldly, 'That's what I keep asking myself – how am I?'

I wanted to put things right. I wanted to say, 'Let's talk about the tombstone and then forget about it forever,' but I couldn't. The way he glared at me was beginning to make me angry. I felt the urge to shake him. On the bedside table there was a peeled mandarin orange that had been halved but left untouched. There will be another time, I kept telling myself. Except that I knew he was dying. He had that aghastness which shows itself, months, often a year, before the actual death. We were getting nowhere. The tension was unbearable, rain splashing down, and he with his head lowered, having a colloquy with himself. I reminded myself how hard-working, how frugal, he had been all his life, never admitting to the loneliness that he must have felt, and I thought, why don't I throw my arms around him and say something? But I couldn't. I simply couldn't. It wouldn't have been true. It would have been false. I knew that he despised me for the falsity of my coming and the falsity of my not bringing the matter up, and that he despised himself equally for having done something irreparable.

'Have you been to the grave?' he asked sharply.

'No, but I'm going this afternoon. I've booked the boatman,' I said.

'You'll find Moira's name and mine on my grand-father's tomb . . . chiselled,' he said.

'Chiselled.' The word seemed to cut through the shafts of suffocating air between us.

I knew that he wanted me to leave.

As it turned out, the trip across the lake was cancelled because the weather was so foul. The boatman deemed it too rough and too dangerous. It was the day of a big horse race and he and his wife were in their front room with the fire lit, the television on, and an open bottle of Tia Maria on a little brass table.

Strange to say, neither Edward's name nor Moira's was on the tombstone when I went to his funeral, on a drizzling wet day that November. The grave had already been dug. 'Ten fellas,' as Jacksie the boatman said, had turned up to do the job. Buckets of water had been bailed out of it, but the clay itself was still wet, with a dark boggy seepage. His coffin would rest on his wife's, hers still new-looking, its varnish undimmed, and, in an exchange of maudlin condolences, women remarked that most likely Moira was in there still, waiting to welcome him.

Underneath his wife's remains were those of his mother, the woman she had quarrelled with and driven out of her home, and down in succession were others – husbands, wives, children, all with their differences silenced. When my turn came, I would rest on Edward's coffin, with runners underneath to cushion the weight. These thoughts were passing through my mind as the priest shook holy water over the grave and three young girls threw in red roses. I did not recognise them. Neighbours' children, I assumed. They threw the roses with a certain theatricality, and one of them blushed fiercely. They might as easily have been at a beauty contest.

When the priest started the Rosary, there were nudges and blatant sighs, as it became clear that he was going to recite the full five decades, and not just one decade, as some priests did. He was in a wheelchair and had to have a boat all to himself. Men had had to support him up the gravel path to the graveyard. Despite his condition, his voice boomed out onto the lake, where the water birds shivered in the rushes, and over it to the main road, where crows had perched in a neat sepulchral line on the telephone wires as the coffin was being removed from the hearse. The mourners answered the Our Fathers and the Hail Marys with a routine drone, and the grave-diggers stood by their shovels, expressionless, witnessing a scene such as they witnessed every other day.

At the end of the prayers, a purple cloth was laid over Edward's coffin, the undertaker tucking it in as if it were a living person that he was putting down to bed. I felt no sorrow, or, to be more precise, I felt nothing, only numbness. I watched a single flake of snow drift through the cold air, discoloured and lonesome-looking.

Most of the people ambled down toward the pier, but a few stayed behind to watch as the men closed the grave. The wreaths and artificial flowers in their glass domes were lifted off the strip of green plastic carpet, which had been temporarily placed over the open grave to lessen the sense of grimness. The gravediggers shovelled hurriedly, gravel and small stones hopping off the coffin and the purple sheath, and finally they unrolled the piece of turf and laid it back where it belonged. Wildflowers of a darkish purple bloomed on graves nearby, but on the strip that had been dug up they had expired. The undertaker, who was full of cheer, said that they would grow again, as the birds scattered seeds all over and flowers of every description sprouted up.

On the way down the steep path, Nurse Gleeson

tugged at my arm as if we were old friends. First it was a slew of compliments about the tweed suit I was wearing, singling out the heather flecks in it, and she said what a pity it was that she was size 18, otherwise I could pass it on to her when I grew tired of it. Then it was my head scarf, an emerald green with other vivid colours, quite inappropriate for a funeral, except that it was the only one I had thrown into my suitcase. She remembered my flying visit to the hospital, had, in fact, gone to get a tray of tea and biscuits, when, holy cripes, on returning to the room, she saw that I had vanished.

'Did he say anything?' I asked.

'Oh, he sang dumb,' she said, then, gripping my arm even tighter, she indicated that there was something important that she needed to impart to me.

A few days before the end, my cousin had asked her for a sheet of notepaper in order to write me a letter. There was a cranberry bowl in the kitchen at home, which he wished me to have, he had said. As it happened, she had found the sheet of paper in the top pocket of his pyjamas after he died, but with nothing written on it.

'The strength gave out,' she said and asked if I knew which bowl it was. I could see it quite clearly, as I had seen it one day, while waiting in his kitchen for a sun shower to pass, rays of sun alighting on it, divesting it of its sheath of brown dust, the red ripples flowing through it, so that it seemed to liquefy, as if it were being newly blown. It had been full of things – screwdrivers, a tiny torch, receipts, and pills for pain. When I admired it, he turned the contents out onto the table and held it in the palm of his hand, proudly, like a chalice of warm wine.

I hoped that the unwritten letter had been an attempt at reconciliation.

Sitting in the boat with a group of friendly people, I could still see the island, shrouded in a veil of thin grey rain. Why, I asked myself, did I want to be buried there? Why, given the different and gnawing perplexities? It was not love and it was not hate but something for which there is no name, because to name it would be to deprive it of its truth.